Dr. Amy Wheatley's Guide to Finding the Perfect Man

—Insist you simply don't have time for dating and men.

—Give in to gentle pressure and accept one blind date. Only one!

—Try to catch your breath when you open the door to see the man of your dreams on your front porch.

—Enlist his help in getting the town matchmakers off both your backs with your pretend-to-date-exclusively plan.

—Realize you *want* to date him exclusively—and more!

—Don't give up when he says he cares for you more than any other woman, but just can't say those three little words....

Dear Reader,

Heartwarming, emotional, compelling...these are all words that describe Harlequin American Romance. Check out this month's stellar selection of love stories, which are sure to delight you.

First, Debbi Rawlins delivers the exciting conclusion of Harlequin American Romance's continuity series, TEXAS SHEIKHS. In *His Royal Prize,* sparks fly immediately between dashing sheikh Sharif and Desert Rose ranch hand Olivia Smith. However, Sharif never expected their romantic tryst to be plastered all over the tabloids—or that the only way to salvage their reputations would be to make Olivia his royal bride.

Bestselling author Muriel Jensen pens another spectacular story in her WHO'S THE DADDY? miniseries with *Daddy To Be Determined,* in which a single gal's ticking biological clock leads her to convince a single dad that he's the perfect man to father her baby. In *Have Husband, Need Honeymoon,* the third book in Rita Herron's THE HARTWELL HOPE CHESTS miniseries, Alison Hartwell thought her youthful marriage to an air force pilot had been annulled, but surprise! Now a forced reunion with her "husband" has her wondering if a second honeymoon couldn't give them a second chance at forever. And Harlequin American Romance's promotion THE WAY WE MET...AND MARRIED continues with *The Best Blind Date in Texas.* Don't miss this wonderful romance from Victoria Chancellor.

It's a great lineup, and we hope you enjoy them all!

Wishing you happy reading,

Melissa Jeglinski
Associate Senior Editor
Harlequin American Romance

THE BEST BLIND DATE IN TEXAS

Victoria Chancellor

TORONTO • NEW YORK • LONDON
AMSTERDAM • PARIS • SYDNEY • HAMBURG
STOCKHOLM • ATHENS • TOKYO • MILAN • MADRID
PRAGUE • WARSAW • BUDAPEST • AUCKLAND

To George and Bonnie Arthur,
the aunt and uncle of my heart.

Acknowledgment:

Special thanks to Dr. Rick Miles,
former Butler High School classmate, friend and small-town doctor, for his expertise, time and encouragement.

ISBN 0-373-16884-5

THE BEST BLIND DATE IN TEXAS

This edition published by arrangement with Harlequin Books S.A.

Visit us at www.eHarlequin.com

Printed in U.S.A.

ABOUT THE AUTHOR

While growing up in Louisville, Kentucky, Victoria Chancellor never realized her vivid imagination meant that she would someday become a writer. Now married to a Texan and settled in a suburb of Dallas, she thoroughly enjoys creating fictional worlds inhabited by characters who deserve a happy ending. When she's not writing, Victoria cares for her "zoo" of three cats, two ferrets, two tortoises, a flock of naturalized ring-necked doves and assorted wild animals who wander onto her patio for dinner each night. She would love to receive letters at P.O. Box 852125, Richardson, TX 75085-2125. Please enclose a SASE for reply.

Books by Victoria Chancellor

HARLEQUIN AMERICAN ROMANCE

844—THE BACHELOR PROJECT
884—THE BEST BLIND DATE IN TEXAS

Amy Jo Wheatley

Mission: Needs a man in her life!
Deadline: Must have date for upcoming medical fund-raiser.
Occupation: Doctor—just like her proud papa!
Characteristics: Responsible, dedicated, intelligent and family oriented.
Candidates To Rule Out: The new guy pumping gas at the Kash 'n Karry. Farmers. And definitely not interested in any feed store employees!
Candidate To Consider: Grayson Phillips—The Best Blind Date in Ranger Springs and the only man interesting enough to date the doctor's daughter.

Grayson Phillips

Mission: Find an eligible female who will make this bachelor forget his own dating rules!
Deadline: Only drawback—hasn't shown any interest in meeting and marrying Ms. Right since he moved to Ranger Springs. Friends say his first wife did a real number on him.
Occupation: Owns Grayson Industries.
Characteristics: Charming, creative and intelligent.
Candidates To Rule Out: Any woman he's dated more than once.
Candidate To Consider: Dr. Amy Jo Wheatley—this doctor's healing touch is just what Texas's most eligible bachelor needs!

Four Square Café

Chapter One

"Amy Jo, you need a man."

Dr. Amy Wheatley loved her dad more than anyone else in this world, but he could be the most single-minded person in all of Texas.

She clamped her teeth shut to keep from firing back a hasty, ill-advised comment. Her father's statement wasn't new; he'd been making similar remarks for about three years, ever since she'd finished her residency. Now that she'd moved back to Ranger Springs, Amy knew she was in for even more pressure to change her title from "Dr." to "Mrs."

"Dad, we've been over this ten-dozen times," she said calmly, hefting another file box on top of the huge old oak desk that would be hers. "I do not need a man in my life. Especially not right now."

She had enough to do just unpacking, opening a bank account and getting reacquainted with the people who would soon be her patients. Coming back to her hometown had been a dream, a goal she hadn't dared voice. She'd vowed she'd stay away, allow her father to continue his medical practice until he decided to retire. But his recent fall had been the perfect excuse to quit the group practice she'd joined in Fort Worth to become her father's partner.

He needed her more than ever before. Now she could contribute to his practice, not just his personal life. As a child she'd baked his favorite brownies and handcrafted cheerful cards when he'd had a bad day. Ever since her mother's death, Amy had played the role of lady of the house. Now she was also a doctor, a fully qualified professional who could shoulder her share of responsibility at the Wheatley Medical Clinic.

Her dad limped into the office where he'd reviewed patient's medical records, written prescriptions and read hundreds of journal articles over his forty years of practicing medicine. Settling into one of the two matching chairs, he gave a big sigh. "Amy Jo, I'm not talkin' about your life, although I know you'll be happier when you settle down with someone special."

Her father gave another dramatic sigh. "No, girl, I'm talkin' about that medical fund-raiser you're goin' to attend in Austin. The fact of the matter is you need a date."

She stopped unpacking and narrowed her eyes. "You didn't mention that when you had me sign up." Apparently he'd found another way to slip a man into her life. Not that she had anything against men…but now was not a good time to start a social life.

"Heck, no. You didn't need a date to sign up, but you're going to be the only one sitting by herself during that big dance."

He'd apparently thought this through, but she

wasn't going to give up easily. If she did, he'd be encouraged in his quest to find her a husband. "Daddy, maybe I don't even need to go. I have a lot to do before I start seeing patients at the clinic a week from Monday. And the donation is the important thing, right? The food isn't usually that great at those hotel dinners, and I don't care much about dancing."

His momentary silence made her look up from the stack of folders. She couldn't miss the spark of devilment in his blue eyes. "What?"

"Maryanne Perkins Bridges is chairin' the shindig."

Amy groaned as she buried her head behind her hands. Maryanne, who'd competed against Amy from the time they met at a junior high track meet, throughout high school and on into college. Maryanne, who'd beaten Amy by two points on the SAT and stolen the interest of Jason Price, the Wimberley High School quarterback. Of all the people from her past, Amy didn't want her old nemesis to see her as the only single young female physician at a charity dinner dance. Or, worse yet, see her name on the list and know she didn't have the nerve to show up in person.

Sinking into her chair, she hid from his watchful eyes behind the box of letters and articles. Darn it, he'd known exactly what to say to make her agree to a blind date.

"But come to think of it, Amy Jo, it wouldn't kill you to go out with some nice young man."

Okay, he was going to be especially persistent today, even though he'd already made his point. She needed to pull out her heavy-duty argument. Amy lifted one eyebrow and challenged, ''Who would that be, Dad? A farmer, a feed store employee or the new guy pumping gas at the Kash 'n' Karry out on the state highway? What happened to your advice that I should hold out for someone successful, charming and handsome?''

Dr. Ambrose Wheatley chuckled, then pushed himself up out of the chair. ''Don't worry about it. I've got just the man in mind. The only one I know good enough to date my baby girl.''

''But just one date, Daddy. That's all I'll agree to.''

''You might change your mind after you meet him.''

''I don't think so.''

''He's a real charmer.''

''One date,'' she stated again.

''Owns his own business, right here in town.''

Amy snorted.

''Everybody likes him.''

Amy shook her head and went back to unpacking. ''He must be a saint,'' she mumbled.

''I heard that,'' he said as he grasped his cane and hobbled toward the door.

''Seriously, Dad, I don't want *you* to get *me* a date for the dance.'' Having her father fix her up just seemed too bizarre. Instead, maybe she should call one of her former colleagues in Fort Worth for a favor.

''Of course you do, Amy Jo. You can't go to the most popular medical event in central Texas all by yourself. I know you've been livin' in the big city for a while, but out here in God's country, a pretty young lady needs a date for a nice dinner and dance.''

Ranger Springs might have changed a little since she'd moved away, but she still couldn't think of one man who would fit the profile of an impressive date—the kind of man her father had just described. She hadn't lived here in eleven years, but she had come back to visit, and as far as she knew, most of the ''good ones'' were already married or had moved away. And, like most small towns, Ranger Springs didn't automatically embrace strangers. Who could her father have in mind?

''Please,'' she whispered, ''not one of my old high school classmates.'' If they were still single around here at thirty, chances were pretty good they had a serious flaw. She could very well find herself attending the fund-raiser arm in arm with a guy whose idea of formal wear was a baby blue tuxedo and a ruffled white shirt.

Maybe her father wouldn't be able to find her a date, despite his assurance he knew just the man. If she were alone, she'd be able to slip away from the fund-raiser without ever having to face Maryanne Perkins Bridges and her rich, successful surgeon husband.

She raised her head and stared at the wall of photos in her father's office. Three generations he'd brought into the world, treated, cured and sometimes eulogized. All of this was hers—her legacy. Could she live up to the legend of Dr. Ambrose Wheatley? Would the citizens of Ranger Springs accept her, as a qualified doctor instead of the teenager who'd written "I love Duran Duran" on the cinder block wall of the high school gym?

Whatever the town thought, her father wanted her to come home to practice medicine. And also to find a nice man, settle down and raise some babies. Amy smiled. She never could say no to her daddy when he really had his heart set on something.

"Just no baby blue tuxedos," she prayed aloud in the Saturday silence of her father's office.

"I heard that," her father said as he shut the door.

AMBROSE WHEATLEY concentrated on negotiating the sidewalk with his cane. He had to use the darned thing for at least four more weeks, until he could remove the walking cast. He'd been darned clumsy to fall down the back stairs. At least it was his left. He could still drive with his right foot.

If a fractured ankle was what it took to get Amy back to town, it was a small price to pay.

Oh, he knew she was afraid of coming into the practice. She thought she might take charge, be a bit too bossy like she'd been when she was a youngster. Sooner or later, she'd figure out he wanted her to take the bit between her teeth. He'd had a great career here in Ranger Springs, but it was time to slow down. Time to let a new generation grab the reins.

He pushed open the door of the Four Square Café just around lunchtime, the familiar tinkling of the bell music to his ears. Now that Amy was back, he'd have plenty of time to eat lunch here whenever he pleased. Not that the food was all that great, although it was darn good most days. What he really wanted to enjoy was the company.

One particular lady.

A smile broke out as he spotted his goal. Seated at their regular table, Thelma Rogers and Joyce Winston had just gotten their coffee when he walked up to the table.

"Ladies," he greeted as he leaned on the cane. The darned walk from his car to the café had him aching.

"Ambrose!" Thelma looked up from her menu of today's specials. "What a pleasant surprise."

He glanced at Joyce, who patted her pretty strawberry blond hair and hardly gave him a second look. He smiled and settled into the chair opposite the beauty store owner and operator.

"I've got a job for you two," he said in a near whisper.

That got their attention. "What kind of job?" the newspaper owner and editor asked.

"A little matchmakin'." Ambrose smiled and leaned a bit closer. "I think my baby girl and our newest eligible bachelor would make quite a strikin' pair, don't you think?"

Joyce smiled and nudged Thelma's side. "I think you're right."

GRAYSON PHILLIPS SENSED the tension building inside of him as he made the turn onto Deer Lick Road. His destination, the modest frame home next to Ranger Springs's medical clinic, was in sight. He had nothing against the street, the house or even the woman inside, but still, his muscles tensed for battle and his breaths came faster, more shallow. He should have become accustomed to the feeling, but instead, he'd begun to resent the experience.

Gray wasn't confronting an enemy or embarking on a dangerous activity. No, he'd been pressured into yet another blind date by resident matchmakers Thelma and Joyce, who had made his social life their exclusive business ever since he'd moved to town last summer.

Not that he'd resisted their efforts in the past. Many of their attempts to find him the perfect woman had been earnest, if misguided, efforts. He had yet to convince the two ladies he wasn't looking for a future Mrs. Phillips. Hell, he'd tried married life, and in his opinion, being single was infinitely more desirable. And, despite a barrage of dates that involved dinners in some of Austin and San Antonio's finest restaurants, charity galas and sporting events, dating was still much less expensive than catering to the whims of a wife.

But mostly, he'd realized just recently, their goal wasn't only fixing him up. No, Thelma and Joyce had targeted him as the ideal blind date for whatever single woman under forty in town had a party, reunion, dance or other social obligation to attend.

His car eased into the driveway where his current—and soon to be one-time—date for the evening awaited. Slowly, aware of each crack in the concrete and each loose piece of gravel, he rolled toward the newly painted house. Apparently Dr. Wheatley—the retiring one, not his daughter—had bought the house years ago with plans to expand his practice someday. Gray had heard in town that the modest two-bedroom dwelling had been fixed up for the new doc.

He'd learned the hard way that the grapevine in Ranger Springs was usually accurate and exceedingly prompt. If he didn't know better, he'd think that they were using some of the high-tech listening devices his company developed and manufactured. If he kissed a woman good-night, the entire downtown area was buzzing with the implications by lunchtime the next day. Thelma and Joyce seemed to be the ring leaders, although Gray had his suspicions that some of the older men who hung out at the Four Square Café were just as guilty.

He would have felt more used if he'd believed the two women were taking advantage of him. They weren't. They simply couldn't believe a single man was happy in his bachelor state. The two old friends believed they had a civic duty to see him matched up with some local woman who possessed the talent, grace or beauty necessary to win his heart.

''Right,'' he muttered as he killed the engine of his silver Lexus. Little did they know how resistant he was finding the ideal mate. He'd loved his ex-wife, Connie, with the passion of youth, then with the settled assurance of married life. Sure, he'd spent much of his time building his invention into a business. He'd never realized she ''suffered'' from his lack of attention or absences. Not until he'd discovered her affair with one of his best friends. One of his *former* best friends.

Much to his surprise, his heart hadn't died when he'd discovered his ex-wife's betrayal, but his pride had suffered a major injury—one he was unwilling to repeat. The experience had reminded him of facts he'd learned from his divorced parents: first, relationships, especially marriages, should never be taken for granted, and second, nothing lasts forever.

His focus for the past four years had been building his company, Grayson Industries, into a high-tech competitor. The move from Dallas to Ranger Springs last year had been a good one. He provided jobs for many who chose to live in the Hill Country, plus his costs were way down since the move. And he was getting settled in a house that suited him on an ideal piece of land overlooking a rugged, winding valley.

Drawing in a deep breath, he ran his hands along the leather-covered steering wheel, letting the texture and shape calm him. He concentrated on everything that was right with his life at this moment: his business, this new town, his single status.

He slipped out of the warm interior of his car, welcoming the blast of cold air that swirled around the house from the north. He ducked his head against the head wind as he followed the cracked concrete walk past the yellow chrysanthemums and orange marigolds. His imported leather shoes made no sound as he climbed the two steps to the front porch. Before ringing the doorbell, he adjusted the lapels of his tux and ran his fingers through his salt-and-pepper hair.

"Showtime," he whispered as he pressed the buzzer.

AMY TOOK A DEEP BREATH, smoothed a hand down the simple lines of her ice blue, raw silk cocktail dress, and pushed out of the chair. She hadn't heard her date arrive, despite sitting in her living room listening intently for the past ten minutes.

Not that she was anxious to meet him, or, for that

matter, to even attend tonight's function in Austin. No, she was simply curious about the man so many had praised as the perfect blind date. After her father had informed her he'd made the arrangements, Amy had gotten rave reviews on the man from everyone she'd met. She couldn't remember any outsider who'd moved into the area who had been so totally accepted by the residents of Ranger Springs and beyond.

What could make this particular man so perfect? And why, unless he had a serious personality flaw or hygiene problem, did he need to go on so many blind dates? From her experience, good-looking, single men who were interested in women could get their own dates. She simply couldn't imagine why everyone from Pastor Carl Schlepinger to the newest clerk at the Kash 'n' Karry sang Grayson Phillips's praises so highly.

Until she opened the door.

She snapped her mouth shut. Standing there gaping like a dead guppy wouldn't give a great first impression to the tall, drop-dead gorgeous man with riveting gray eyes and dark hair liberally shot with silver. His wide shoulders more than did justice to the well-cut tuxedo and perfectly tailored white shirt.

No ruffles. No baby blue polyester.

"Miss Wheatley?" the Adonis at her door asked. "I'm Gray Phillips."

"Dr. Wheatley," she said automatically, her voice husky from disuse.

"Of course. My mistake," he replied, his sculpted features and intelligent eyes giving nothing away. "I've met your father, and please, I mean this as no disrespect to him, but you hardly resemble my only experience with a small-town doctor.''

''I'll take that as a compliment,'' she said, trying to get her brain and mouth working in sync as she stepped out of his way. ''Please, come in. And call me Amy.''

As he walked past her, she noticed that he smelled as good as he looked. So much for her theory on over-thirty single men, personal hygiene and blind dates.

She led him into the living room—not that there was much leading to be done. The front door opened into the room without so much as a half wall to divide the space. New beige carpet covered the floor, and the walls had been painted a pleasing eggshell, but there was only so much a person could do in the week and a half she'd been in town. Decorating hadn't been high on her list of priorities, so the black leather sofa and matching chair she'd moved with her, along with a couple of nondescript tables, sat abandoned against the walls.

''I'm afraid I haven't settled in much,'' she explained as she rubbed her hands against the chill of the November air that entered along with her date for the evening. ''Can I get you something to drink?''

''No, thank you.''

In what she was sure was a case of extremely good manners, he barely glanced at her plain-but-tidy home. His personal scrutiny made her mildly uncomfortable, as if she wanted to check her dress for wrinkles or her shoes for an errant piece of tissue. But despite her reaction, his expression never wavered from the polite interest he'd shown from the first.

"I'll just get my coat, then," she said, motioning toward the tiny closet near the front door.

As she grasped the wooden hanger, she felt his presence behind her. An unexpected chill slithered up her spine. She couldn't blame this reaction on the uncommonly cold weather.

"You're shivering," he said, taking the wool-and-cashmere blend coat from her hands. "Allow me."

His warmth enveloped her as she slid her arms into the sleek, cool satin lining. Unfortunately, she still felt just as shivery. She wrapped her arms around herself. "I suppose I'm not adjusting well to autumn. Except for this cold snap, the temperatures have been above normal."

"How can you, in Texas? Warm one day, cold the next." He made the comment without derision, just as polite as ever. So far, he was the perfect date, even when she'd resorted to talking about the weather to hide her unexpected reaction to him.

"You're not from the Lone Star State?" she asked as she belted her coat. She stepped around him to retrieve her purse and gloves from the living room.

"Actually, I'm from Dallas, so as a native, I can indulge in a little mild criticism."

Amy smiled at his rationale. "I know what you mean. We can say what we want, but just let some Yankee belittle our state..."

Grayson Phillips smiled. "Shall we go? I understand you'd like to show off a bit for the folks in Austin."

Amy stopped beside the front door, her mouth gaping once again. "Who told you that?" Her lips thinned as she frowned. "No, let me guess. You've been talking to my father."

"I saw him at the bank yesterday."

"The man talks entirely too much."

"He's a charmer."

"He's a meddling old...never mind." Amy squared her shoulders and clasped her purse to her side. "I'm sorry if you feel railroaded into this. I'd understand if you didn't want to go."

"On the contrary, Dr. Amy," he said, a flash of real amusement in his silvery eyes. "I wouldn't miss it for the world."

Great looks and humor, too. As he graciously escorted her toward his luxury car, Amy realized that was why Grayson Phillips really was the best blind date in Texas.

DR. AMY WHEATLEY WASN'T quite what he'd expected, Gray acknowledged as he pulled out of Ranger Springs onto the state highway. For one thing, no one had mentioned she was beautiful. Descriptions he'd heard had focused on her achievements in high school, college and medical school rather than her shining dark brown hair and lively blue eyes. Her father, and the rest of the community, for that matter, were very proud of their small-town girl.

Not just beautiful, though. She was also feminine and gave the impression of being slightly vulnerable. She'd obviously been trying to be as polite as he when he'd first arrived at her door. But during the few minutes they'd gotten acquainted at her home, she'd shown a wide range of emotions, from surprise to shyness to exasperation over her father's meddling. While Gray had perfected the control he exerted over his own emotions and expressions, he appreciated Amy's honest responses.

"I've heard a little about your new facility in town. What exactly do you produce?" she asked.

"Basically, Grayson Industries makes high-tech surveillance devices. Our main market is government as opposed to consumers who want to listen to what their neighbors are saying."

He risked a glance at her. She appeared surprised, then perplexed. "You mean my neighbors could be eavesdropping on me? Or, worse yet, the government?"

Gray chuckled. "The technology has been around for years, so we're not providing any less privacy to the average citizen than already exists. My company simply makes smaller, more flexible instruments for specialty surveillance situations."

"You mean like spies?"

Gray smiled. He'd heard this all before, but he knew Amy's worries were real to her. "There really aren't too many James Bonds out there."

"No, but isn't industrial espionage on the rise?"

"It's getting more sophisticated, but with computers and the Internet, more violations are occurring via online theft than through listening devices."

"Hmm." She paused as she looked at the fading sunset. "Still, doesn't it worry you that your products will enable some criminals to steal secrets?"

"No more than if I made modems that allowed some hacker to access the Internet," he answered, negotiating a series of turns as they traveled north through the rolling hills. "I'm not trying to justify what I do, because I don't see anything wrong with developing the technology to have an edge over those who would like to harm our country."

"It's kind of creepy, though, don't you think?"

"Not when you invented it," he said, smiling at her through the gloom of near darkness. "Don't worry, though. I promise I didn't plant any bugs in your house, nor will I sit outside in an unmarked van with an earplug and a big antenna."

"That's comforting—I think," she said, partially in jest, he assumed. "So, what brought you to Ranger Springs?"

"Available labor, a good cost of living and quality schools. We'd been in Dallas for several years, but the competition for skilled workers up there is crazy. I decided I could take advantage of the labor market down here and train our employees in the skills they needed. Most of our engineers and research staff relocated after visiting the Hill Country."

"Did you bring them down to visit when the bluebonnets and Indian paintbrush were blooming?"

"Of course," he answered with a grin. Few areas of the world surpassed the beauty of the Texas Hill Country in the spring, when the blue and red flowers dotting the hills resembled an Impressionist's canvas. When birds soared through the sky and filled the day with song, and the air smelled so fresh and clear a person wanted to join in the singing.

Darkness descended as Gray drove through the rural rolling hills, then into the traffic of Dripping Springs and the outskirts of Austin. Inside the car, he felt isolated from the world, enveloped in the scent of Amy's light perfume and the softness of her voice. She would have a great bedside manner, he told himself, then stopped his wayward thought. He wasn't getting anywhere near Amy Wheatley's bed, nor she near his. One date with any woman was enough. Two and they started expecting commitment. A month, and they were picking out rings.

He wasn't about to make the same mistake twice, especially now when he had everything he'd worked to achieve.

He knew the hotel where the fund-raiser was taking place, so he pulled into valet parking with time to spare.

"Ready to knock them dead?"

"I'm supposed to save lives, not take them," she quipped as the attendant opened her car door.

Gray waited until they passed through the glass doors before he leaned close to her ear. "Believe me, you, in that dress, could cause a few heart attacks."

She laughed and shook her head. "Grayson Phillips, has anyone ever told you you're a smooth-talking devil?"

How could he answer that question without admitting his greatest strength, and perhaps his biggest weakness? He'd learned at a young age that most people—especially his successful parents—weren't interested in how he *really* felt. Outward appearances made all the difference in the world. So he'd learned to become what people expected, and later, what they wanted. Most women wanted a suave, sophisticated date who focused all his attention on them.

So he simply smiled and answered, "That sounds like something your father would say."

She cocked her head and wrinkled her brow. "You know, you're right. Maybe there's more of him in me than I realized."

"We are a product of our environment," he said, thinking of his own divorced parents and his ex-wife. What had he learned from those experiences? The notion sobered him, and he put on another smile to cover his darker thoughts.

With a light touch to Amy's arm, he stopped her in the wide, carpeted hallway leading to the ballroom. "Are you ready?"

"Unless I can pull a good reason out of a hat in the next five seconds."

"Sorry, but I'm not wearing a hat."

"Then I guess we'll have to go in."

He took a step forward, but her touch on his forearm stopped him. "Gray, I want to thank you again for being my escort this evening. I could have come alone, but my father—"

"Wanted you to have a good time." Gray smiled, genuinely this time. "I understand."

He slipped her coat off her shoulders and handed it to the coat-check attendant outside the ballroom door. "You can introduce me to all your colleagues. I promise not to bore them with technical jargon and high-tech market analysis. I'll try to be on my most charming behavior."

"Oh," she said, looking him over in a very feminine manner that made his insides tighten and his chest expand, "I never doubted you for a moment."

Chapter Two

Despite the tension she'd experienced upon entering the room full of medical professionals from central Texas, Amy had a good time during the dinner dance. The entertainment, a reunited band from the early seventies, had been upbeat and humorous. And the man who'd been beside her all evening had been a major factor in making her relax and enjoy the fund-raiser.

The only truly tense moment she'd experienced was when she and Gray literally bumped into Maryanne and her husband during a rousing Texas two-step. Amy hadn't seen her former classmate for two years. Their last encounter had been at Maryanne's society wedding to a middle-aged surgeon, Dr. Paul Bridges. Amy hadn't wanted to attend, but in the end, the invitation was just too intriguing to pass up.

Sure enough, Maryanne had outdone herself. The event had been spectacular. The bride was stunning in a dress whose cost probably equaled Amy's entire student loan for medical school. And Maryanne hadn't gloated too much about achieving everything she'd ever desired. Just a few subtle hints about Amy's single status and group practice.

She sighed. At least tonight they hadn't had time to "chat."

"What's wrong?" Gray asked as they waited for his car to be brought around.

"Just thinking about old times," she answered with a smile. "You know how it is when you haven't seen someone in a while."

"And she still looks stunning," he added.

Amy blinked. "Did you think so?"

Gray chuckled. "Yes, but in a rather contrived manner. I doubt that particular shade of blond occurs in nature." His gaze became more direct, his mood more serious. "She's not as naturally beautiful as you."

She felt her cheeks heat and her heart flutter. "Thank you for the kind words, but being outrageous isn't part of your date duties for the evening."

"I thought I was being rather sedate in my compliments," he said as he tipped the parking attendant. "I may be a smooth-talking devil, as you said earlier, but I'm also a man who knows a lovely woman when he sees one."

She eased inside the car, pulling her coat tight against the chill. "I'm flattered."

He took her hand and placed a kiss right above her knuckles. His silvery, hooded eyes sparkled in the reflected light of the hotel portico. "I'm glad."

Amy hadn't felt this giddy from a man's attentions in a long, long time. Too long. She simply hadn't had the time or the inclination to start a meaningful relationship in what seemed like ages.

No wonder she found Gray's flattery and old-fashioned gallantry so appealing. That, combined with his reputation as the perfect date, was enough to get any woman's attention.

Gray pulled the Lexus into the crawl of downtown Austin traffic. "The night's still fairly young. Would you enjoy going to one of my favorite spots for an after-dinner drink and a little light jazz?"

Amy thought about it for a moment. She hadn't planned on anything other than the fund-raiser, but Gray was right; the clock on the dash read only ten-thirty. It wasn't like her father was waiting in the doorway, tapping his foot. As a matter of fact, he'd probably be tickled pink if she stayed out half the night!

Besides, Gray had been a gracious and charming date; the least she could do was accompany him to a favorite haunt. She didn't know how often he traveled the distance from Ranger Springs to Austin for an evening out.

"Sure. That sounds lovely."

Gray nodded, then guided the car through frequent stops and unending road construction. Amy lost track of where they were heading, letting her head fall back and relax against the cool leather. She could get used to this type of luxury...but not on a small-town doctor's salary. In another two years, if she was careful, she might upgrade to a small SUV, but not anything this fancy. Mainly, she needed reliable transportation. Her father still believed in making house calls when absolutely necessary.

Strange how different the practice of medicine was here than in Fort Worth. Oh, the ailments would be the same, Amy knew. But the attitude, the atmosphere, couldn't be more opposite. She welcomed the sense of community and the support of her father to help her make the transition. She only hoped she was up to the task. She was a good doctor; she knew her abilities and training wouldn't let her down. But would she be accepted on her own, or forever compared to her father?

"You look pensive," Gray observed, breaking into her thoughts.

"I was just thinking about my practice. I'll start seeing patients on Monday. We arranged the schedule at the clinic so I've had a few days to unpack and get settled in. I'm looking forward to helping out my father, but I also know I'll be compared to him."

"That's inevitable, I suppose, but I'm sure most people will welcome you as both a doctor and a returning member of the community."

"I hope so. I've been away a long time."

"Are you afraid they'll still think of you as a child?"

Amy nodded. "That's part of it. The other issues are what any doctor faces—style, reputation and personality."

"I can't imagine you'll have any problem there," Gray said, giving her an appreciative, thorough perusal as he stopped at a red light.

Amy warmed at both his compliment and the attention. "Thank you. Of course, you don't know a thing about my medical skills."

"I have faith that you're a good doctor. From what I've heard about your father, he wouldn't have just anyone as a partner."

"I hope you're right."

"I usually am," he said with a smile as he pulled the car back into traffic.

"All that and modest too," Amy said, then chuckled.

Gray reached over and squeezed her hand. "You'll be fine."

"I hope so. I really want to make a future here, and I'd like the community to accept me before my hair turns as gray as my father's."

Gray chuckled. "I don't think you have anything to worry about, at least not for a few dozen years."

"I'm pushing thirty," Amy announced. Besides the big birthday coming up, she'd recently begun to hear her biological clock ticking. Of course, she wasn't about to mention that tidbit to her father. He was already insisting that she find a nice man and settle down. If he started thinking about grandkids, she'd never get a moment's peace!

"And I've already seen my thirty-fourth. I suppose the difference is that I don't feel a lot of pressure from anyone to do anything I don't want to do."

"Lucky you," Amy said with a little chuckle. "If you ever get lonely for unsolicited advice, just let me know. I'll send my father over to harass you."

Gray laughed as he pulled into the parking lot of a two-story brick building with few markings on the outside. A neon beer sign lighted one window and an old-fashioned painted sign swung over the sidewalk in the light, cool breeze.

"I know it doesn't look like much," he said as he shut off the engine, "but trust me. The music is great."

She did trust him, Amy realized as she pulled her coat tight and swung her legs out of the Lexus. She'd only known the man a few hours, yet already they'd learned they had several things in common: both were only children; both loved springtime in the Hill Country; both preferred to eat their salad with their meal instead of finishing it first. Not a bad start for a blind date.

The interior of the club was dark and slightly smoky, but not overwhelmingly so. Gray took her hand as they weaved through small tables and chairs, most occupied by an eclectic crowd of college students, upscale patrons and serious middle-age jazz aficionados. His hand was warm and strong, and she felt her heart rate increase ever so slightly from just a simple touch.

He found a half-circle booth of red tufted vinyl that had seen better days. All part of the ambiance, she supposed. When Gray stopped and let his hand ease away, she felt the absence of his touch more than she would have thought. After all, they weren't really dating. He'd only touched her a few times, and very casually. Still, she wished she could have rested her hand in his for a while longer.

"Would you like me to take your coat?" he asked.

"Thank you." He helped her ease it off her shoulders and arms, then folded it across the back of the booth. Again, she felt his nearness, warmth and strength.

"What would you like to drink? The service here isn't great, so I usually go up to the bar to order."

"I think a Baileys would be nice."

Gray nodded. "I'll be right back."

Amy scooted into the booth, then debated how far to move over. If she didn't go very far in the half circle, Gray might think she wanted him to sit very close beside her on the outside. On the other hand, if she sat near the edge, he'd be forced to sit across from her. They'd have to shout to be heard over the music. Not a good choice.

In the end, she moved to the middle of the red vinyl bench, adjusted the hem of her icy blue dress, and put a welcoming smile on her face.

"Two Baileys," he announced, placing them on the table with the finesse of the best waiter. He noticed her position in the booth, smiled and eased around to the left so he sat close, but not crowded against her.

"Thanks."

Gray settled back against the cushions. "From what you said earlier, I get the impression your father tends to give his advice rather freely."

Amy laughed. "You could say that. Don't get me wrong—he's a great dad. He's just extremely opinionated and believes the world would work a whole lot better if everyone followed his orders."

"And I take it your orders included returning to your hometown."

"No," Amy said, frowning as she remembered their conversations while she was in medical school. "He never insisted I join him at the clinic. He just had a lot of advice on how a good doctor practiced medicine."

"That's good, I suppose. He has a lot of experience."

"Yes, but that's not the opinion he's been giving me for the last three years."

"Oh?"

Amy blushed. She shouldn't tell Gray this, but he was so easy to talk to, she found the words slipping out. "He wants me to find a nice man and settle down." Amy sipped her drink, then paused. "Not that I meant anything by that remark. I mean, just because you got railroaded into taking me to this fund-raiser, I don't want you to think...Oh, I'm not explaining this well, am I?"

Gray chuckled. "No explanation needed. I know how parents can be. I've heard the same thing from mine a time or two, especially before..."

"Before what?" Amy asked, leaning forward.

He shrugged. "Before my marriage."

"Oh." No one had mentioned he was married. Or had been married. Her father wouldn't fix her up with a married man.

"After the divorce, they quit pestering me."

"I see." She wanted to say more, but the band chose that moment to start a new set. The deep thrumming of strings reverberated through the club, followed by the wail of a saxophone. When she looked at Gray, she saw him watching the band, but a slight frown creased his forehead.

THE BAND TOOK A BREAK, leaving the club in sudden silence. Gray was surprised to discover he wanted to explain more about what he'd admitted—and the implications of being single. He rarely talked about the divorce, and never discussed the reasons for the breakup. Somehow, with Amy, the words seem to come naturally.

On most blind dates, the women had done most of the talking. Perhaps because she was a doctor and accustomed to listening to her patients, Amy had a quiet, observant manner he found refreshing.

"I didn't mean to drop the fact I'm divorced on you like that," he said. "It's been four years, so I don't think about my marital status much."

"If you date as much as I've heard, I suspect you remember that you're single," she said with a cheeky grin.

"I don't date all that much," he defended, "and yes, I'm definitely single—and planning on staying that way."

"Mmm. Messy divorce?"

"Messy marriage."

"Oops. Sorry."

"Don't be. I'm better off now than ever. But the experience did leave me with a rather bitter taste for tying the knot again."

"I understand. I'm certainly not ready to rush into anything either. I'm going to have my hands full getting the clinic back to full speed as quickly as possible."

Gray hesitated, but Amy had left the perfect opening for him to explain something. One of his rules. He liked her, more than anyone he'd met recently, but she needed to understand how he operated so she wouldn't be hurt.

"Amy, I've really had a great time tonight, and I think you're a wonderful person. I don't usually say this outright, but I'm going to in this case." He drew in a fortifying breath. "I don't know what you've heard about me around town, but I have an unspoken rule."

"About dating?"

"Yes. You see, I never have a second date with anyone."

She sat up, her eyes showing surprise. "Never?"

"Not since I moved to Ranger Springs."

"So that's why you've dated so many different women."

"Whatever Thelma and Joyce arrange," he said, taking another sip of his drink.

"Thelma and Joyce? But I thought my father arranged this evening."

Gray shrugged. "Maybe he did, through my unofficial personal dating service."

"He's in cahoots with those two women."

Gray smiled at Amy's accusing words, softened by the love shining from her eyes and the fondness evident in her voice. She'd complained earlier about her father's meddling, but she obviously cared for him very much. "Perhaps."

"I'm going to have a serious talk with the man."

Gray shook his head. "Not on my account. Like I said, I've really enjoyed this evening." He certainly didn't want to be the cause of any problems between Amy and her father.

"But you want me to know there won't be a repeat."

He jerked his thoughts away from Amy's relationship with her father to the one she'd never have with *him.* "Yes. You see, I realized early on that if I dated any woman more than once, the gossipmongers would jump on the news. And then if I didn't date another one but once, some perfectly nice woman would get her feelings hurt."

"That's very thoughtful of you," Amy said carefully, "but doesn't having only one date with any woman cramp your style?"

Gray laughed. "Not really. Like I said, I'm busy with the move of my company, hiring and training employees and expanding our markets. I don't have that much time for a social life."

He hadn't had one in so long, as a matter of fact, he rarely missed the quiet, shared evenings, dinner conversations with someone well known, the feel of a woman's warm flesh after making love. At least he told himself he didn't miss those things. If he thought about how long he'd been abstinent—nearly two years—he might not be as cheerful.

His last relationship, a comfortable, no-pressure affair with an equally career-minded lawyer he'd known socially for years, had ended before he'd decided to move from Dallas. He hadn't been serious about the woman; he'd just fallen into the mutually satisfying affair after his divorce.

Strange, but Amy's assertions she wasn't looking for a long-term relationship, especially one with a husband and children, echoed his own position now. He wasn't looking for the complications a family would bring…and yet, the longer he lived in this close-knit community, the less objectionable he found the idea…in theory.

Gray mentally shook his head. He had no business thinking along those lines. Especially not while he was out on his *one date* with Amy Wheatley.

"So what do you do when Thelma and Joyce fix you up? Do you turn them down?"

"Well, I haven't so far, but I may have to start. They do seem to be getting a little persistent in their efforts."

"Poor Gray," Amy said with a smile. "So many women, so little time."

A problem many men would gladly accept, he knew. And yet he found the process tedious. Boring. All those words some men applied to their permanent relationship. To married life.

He had to stop thinking along those lines. He was still in performance mode, still giving yet another woman a perfect date.

Gray grabbed her glass and gave his best effort at acting the role, a ferociously teasing frown. "One more remark like that and you won't get another drink."

"One more outrageous revelation from you and I'm going to need another drink." She held up her hand. "Seriously, a soft drink would be great."

He laughed as he left the booth, but sobered upon approaching the bar. Amy was a unique woman. He'd really enjoyed this evening, despite the fact he'd started thinking about certain taboo subjects. Despite the fact she made him want things that weren't in his immediate future.

Perhaps it was best that they wouldn't be repeating the experience.

"ONE MORE DANCE TO close out the evening?" he asked as she listened to the soulful sounds.

One more chance to stand close to this one-date

bachelor, to tempt herself with what couldn't happen? They'd danced at the fund-raiser, but in a more structured setting and style. Here, on the minuscule dance floor, Amy had a feeling Gray would let his guard down just a little.

One more chance to tempt herself? "Why not?"

He led her onto the parquet floor, pulling her closer than he had at the fancy hotel. One hand closed warmly over hers, while the other slid down her back to rest low on her waist. She felt the heat and imprint of his fingers through the silk of her dress, just as she felt his chest brush against hers. Their legs moved in rhythm, with only his pants and her skirt touching.

For just a moment, she longed for him to pull her close, until there was no polite distance between them. Until she could feel the beating of his heart against her breast and experience the sensation of his hot breath on her neck.

But such romantic, physical contact would be ludicrous. She wasn't into one-night stands, and Gray had been honest about his dating rules.

When the song ended, she let out a sigh. Someone slowly turned up the lights until she could see Gray's pensive expression. But then, as he always seemed to do, he schooled his features into a neutral, pleasant expression as he gazed down at her.

Then her stomach rumbled.

Not just a tiny little sound, but a clearly discernible signal that she was hungry. Starved, in fact.

Gray chuckled. "I did mention earlier that you were eating like a bird."

"Prime rib isn't my favorite, and even if it were,

I'm not sure I could have forced down another bite of the shoe leather we were served."

"To tell you the truth, I could use some food myself." He raised his arm and glanced at his watch. "It's after midnight, so that means we can officially have breakfast."

"Officially?"

"Absolutely."

"I suppose you know another great place."

"Of course," he replied with a grin. The glint in his silvery eyes told her the breakfast spot would be as unusual as his choice of nightclubs.

Amy smiled as he led her off the dance floor. They had no future together, but apparently their one-time date wasn't quite finished yet.

GRAY PULLED THE LEXUS to a stop and cut the headlamps. He didn't need artificial light to see the structure in front of him. He'd been coming here for years. This place was one of the biggest reasons he'd decided to move to the Hill Country.

He would have had some explaining to do, except that Amy had gone to sleep almost as soon as they'd settled into the car. He'd been free to drive as he wished, setting up what he hoped would be a good surprise. He'd never taken another woman to this place, but if he was to have only one date with Amy, he wanted her to spend just a little time here.

In the bucket seat across from him, she stirred. Beneath her open coat, he noticed how the pale blue silk dress stretched over her breasts as she shifted in the seat. Amy Wheatley was not only an intelligent, beautiful woman, but she was witty and pleasant. More than pleasant, she was desirable.

He wasn't going to act on his desire, though. One date was all he'd have with Amy, no matter how much he'd like to begin a relationship. If he allowed himself to get involved with her, eventually one of them would get hurt. He wasn't going to get married again, and the good citizens of Ranger Springs would expect him to ask Dr. Ambrose Wheatley for his daughter's hand before long.

Gray looked out the windshield to the darkness. How often he'd come here, looking for answers. Tonight there were no answers to this unexpected dilemma.

He knew Amy wasn't the kind of woman who wanted a clandestine affair, which is all either of them could afford. They couldn't openly flaunt a sexual relationship, or even sneak around like a couple of teenagers for long. Not in a small town. Her reputation as a competent physician would suffer, and his as an upstanding businessman would be null and void.

No, there wasn't any way they could have a relationship. For tonight, however, they could have a great breakfast. He'd take her home, explain again that he didn't do second dates and say that he'd see her around town.

Such a bland statement of the potential he sensed for a mature, mutually satisfying relationship between two adults.

"Gray?"

He schooled his features, then turned to his passenger. "We're here."

"Where?" She sat up and rubbed her eyes. "Oh, it looks like they're closed."

Gray raised his key ring. "Not to me."

"You have a key to a restaurant?" Her sexy voice sounded sleepy and confused—a potent combination.

Gray smiled, anticipating her surprise when she discovered where they were. "Come on."

He walked around the Lexus while Amy belted her coat and gathered her purse. When she swung her legs out of the car, he again admired her long, shapely calves and narrow feet, set off by high heels and pale, glittery hose.

"Gray, where are we?"

He placed his hand under her elbow. The gravel crunched under their impractical shoes as they walked to the porch. Overhead, a billion stars competed with the half moon to light the crisp night air.

"I know you were probably expecting a restaurant, but in all honesty, I make the best breakfast you'll find anywhere."

Amy stopped, her eyes showing some lingering, sleep-induced confusion. "Where are we?"

"At my cabin on Lake Buchanan," he said carefully.

She looked around at the rural setting. "I thought we'd be going to something like a diner in Austin."

"My omelettes are much better."

She closed her eyes and took a deep breath of the crisp, clear air. "This is much nicer. No rowdy teenagers. No smokers in the next booth."

"I'm glad you like it. The view is beautiful during the day." Not that he'd bring her back here to see it, he reminded himself. Again, he felt a hollow ache when he realized he and Amy wouldn't be dating. "My uncle used to bring me here when I was a kid. I bought it from him when he couldn't keep it up any longer."

"You're a very nice man," she said, her voice soft and throaty in the quiet, cold night.

Chills ran up his spine, but had nothing to do with the weather and everything to do with the woman standing before him. "Thank you, but my motives were also selfish. I love coming here to relax."

Amy shrugged, hugging her arms around her. "Well, since I need to find another compliment you'll accept, I could also mention that you're a good dancer."

"That one I'll take, on the condition I have an equally talented partner," he said, slipping his hand beneath her elbow as he guided her toward the cabin. "I'm also a damn good cook."

"I'll be the judge of that," she said just before her tummy rumbled again.

Chapter Three

Amy watched the pale streak of lavender widen and turn to dusky pink as Gray pulled his Lexus to a stop in front of her house. Her brain told her she was a fully grown woman with every right to come home whenever she chose, but the little girl who'd grown up in Ranger Springs whispered that she was going to get in trouble. She half expected to see her father come out of the clinic with a cup of coffee in one hand and a disapproving frown on his face.

Not now, she reminded herself. As long as she was out "finding herself a man," he'd probably offer them both a cup of coffee, a big grin on his lined, dear face.

"We managed to make a night and a morning of it," she said softly after he'd turned off the engine and the quiet of dawn surrounded them. Omelettes had turned into coffee and more conversation in the cozy cabin, until suddenly they'd both realized the drive back to Ranger Springs was well over an hour—and dawn was approaching.

"Are you sorry?"

"No, not at all. I had a wonderful time."

He reached for her hand and Amy's heart began to race. "I've never taken anyone there before."

"Then I'm honored."

"I can't take you there again."

"I know," she whispered. She actually felt an ache in the region of her heart, but she knew the condition wasn't medical. No, this was much more emotional. Too emotional for either of them.

"I've told you my rule against dating anyone twice, but when I'm alone with you, the restriction sounds foolish."

"It's your life, Gray. You have to make your own rules."

His fingers caressed the back of her hand. "But that's just it, Amy. As far as my personal life goes, I feel like I'm not making my own rules. I'm marching to the drums of a certain two ladies."

Amy smiled. She knew exactly what he meant. Her father was insistent, but she could tell him no. She didn't have to worry about acceptance. Even if she didn't settle down, her dad would still love her. Gray obviously wanted social acceptance, and wasn't sure how his refusal to cooperate with Thelma and Joyce would be perceived by the citizens of Ranger Springs.

"Thelma and Joyce can be quite demanding," Amy sympathized.

"Don't I know it," Gray said, shaking his head. "Sometimes I wish..."

"What?"

He paused, and she wondered if he would answer. Perhaps she shouldn't have asked, but he was so easy to talk to.

"That I'd never put myself out there as someone looking for a date," he finally said. "This all started when I needed to attend a function in San Antonio and made an innocent comment about being too busy with my business to ask anyone. Before I knew it, my social calendar was posted on the courthouse wall."

Amy laughed at his exaggeration. "We don't have a courthouse."

"Then they probably had it printed as an insert to the menu at the Four Square Café. That seems to be where they do most of their plotting."

Amy silently agreed. The local café had been a meeting place for two generations. "You make them sound diabolical."

Gray shook his head. "No, really, they're sweet, wonderful ladies. They've just taken me on as their favorite cause."

"Well, now that I'm back in town, perhaps they'll ease up on you. My father will no doubt be looking all over the place for someone to marry his little girl. I'm sure he'll get Thelma and Joyce to help him."

Amy didn't mention that they'd probably already discussed her and Gray in the context of happily-ever-after. Gray apparently hadn't taken their one date to that next, albeit huge, step. She wasn't about to bring up that subject! Perhaps in this one case, ignorance of the degree of matchmaking was bliss.

Gray assumed a serious expression and brought her hand to his lips. "My sympathies," he said, perfectly deadpan.

Amy laughed until tears came to her eyes. "Oh,

Gray, you really are the perfect blind date. No wonder those ladies are so good at fixing you up.''

''I'm going to have to do something soon, because after tonight, no other date will measure up.''

Amy broke eye contact, embarrassed at his praise, even if he did tend to exaggerate. ''Thank you. The feeling is mutual.''

Out on the road, a noisy truck rolled past. Amy glanced over her shoulder, then groaned as the vehicle slowed to a stop. Joyce's nephew, Lester Boggs, peered through the rosy dawn at Gray's Lexus. Even from a distance of several dozen yards, she imagined she could see his pig eyes squinting to see inside the car.

''We've been caught,'' she whispered, turning back to Gray as the old pickup slowly rumbled past. Lester worked at the feed store. By lunchtime, everyone would know Gray was parked in her driveway at dawn.

Gray watched the truck drive away, his expression thoughtful. Pensive. She wondered what he might be thinking. Did he resent being ''caught'' in her driveway? Was he worried about his own reputation?

''Want to really give them something to talk about?'' he finally asked.

''No!'' Besides, Lester was already gone.

''You're right. Kissing you would be a bad idea.''

Her eyes widened, her heart thumped in her chest, as he leaned closer. ''A terrible idea.''

''One of the worst ones I've had in the past twelve hours or so.''

''You're so right,'' she barely managed to whisper before his lips covered hers.

She'd been kissed before. Dozens of times. Perhaps never under just these circumstances, though. That might account for the way her heart was racing, the way her mind spun out of control as his lips sealed over hers and his tongue swirled with wicked, dark promises. Or maybe she was just exhausted. That might account for how she felt dizzy and short of breath. But all she knew for sure was that kissing Grayson Phillips was the most exciting, the most risky, event in her recent history. She responded with pent-up desire and unknown longing, until they were both breathing fast and shallow when the kiss ended.

She sighed as he pulled away, then slowly opened her lids. Pale light made his silvery eyes even more luminous. The early hour gave new meaning to "five o'clock shadow" on his lean cheeks and sculpted chin. She wanted to run her fingers through his salt-and-pepper hair, and pull his deliciously talented mouth back to hers.

"We won't go out again," he said softly, with just a tinge of regret, as his gaze caressed her face.

"I know. You were clear."

"It's the only way. Neither one of us wants the kind of relationship this town would expect from two upstanding citizens."

"You're right." Her voice sounded a bit thin, as though she didn't quite believe her own words. But Gray was correct; there was no future for them. At least, not now. Maybe later, after they were more established... If they didn't find someone else in the meantime.

No, that was ridiculous. She wasn't looking for anyone. Not now, when she'd already discovered the one man who took her breath away. How could another man compare to Gray? And what about his romantic future? Gray would have to make his own decisions.

"I'd better go in," she said as he gazed at her in silence.

"I know." He ran his hand along her hair, brushing her cheek and lightly tracing the shell of her ear. "I had a wonderful time tonight, Dr. Amy Wheatley."

"And I'm very glad you were my blind date," she whispered, the ache in her chest intensifying. Before she did or said something extremely stupid, she pulled her coat tight around her, grabbed her purse, and ran for the safety of her tiny house.

SHRUGGING OUT OF HIS tux jacket, Gray focused his attention on the sky stretching one hundred eighty degrees before him.

The dawn sky was still shaded in pinks and corals. A beautiful morning, but he felt as isolated and alone as this house.

Strange. He'd never felt lonely in this house before. *Before last night.*

He'd built on a hill overlooking a winding valley that was bisected by a stream each spring and fall. A narrow ribbon of water remained, courtesy of last week's rain. This past summer, when the house had been newly finished, the stream had been as dry as the rest of the Texas landscape.

Gray had designed this house, with the help of a San Antonio architect, to reflect his new life. Clean and devoid of distractions, they'd included both natural materials and technological marvels. The wood, glass and rock structure rose from the hill as though it had been here for years.

That's the way Gray wanted to be perceived. Permanent, stable, unobtrusive. He'd wanted to blend into the community, putting down a strong foundation for years to come.

For his company, Gray reminded himself. Some men built to pass along their legacy to their child. He had no children, no wife, to inherit. Grayson Industries was as close as he might ever have to a family. His choice, at least for the time being, he acknowledged. He had nothing against family...children in concept. But he didn't want a wife. He didn't want someone to dangle the promise of happily-ever-after in front of him, then jerk it away just when he'd begun to believe.

Gray jammed his hands into his trouser pockets as a headache threatened. Why had Connie's betrayal hurt so much? Why was it still coloring his perception of his future? He wasn't sure; he wasn't a psychologist or psychiatrist, nor did he intend to visit one. Hell, he wasn't even sure his attitude was a problem.

His desire for Dr. Amy Wheatley...now *that* was a problem.

With a sigh, he headed upstairs for his bedroom. He'd been up for twenty-four hours. With a little luck and a couple of aspirin, he'd be able to sleep a few hours before going back to the office. He just hoped he didn't dream of a certain brunette with intelligent blue eyes, soft smiles and even softer lips. He'd had his time with Amy Wheatley. Now he had to face his days without her, because she definitely believed in happily ever after.

"THE BEST DEFENSE IS A good offense," Amy told herself as she pulled her car to a stop in front of Joyce's beauty shop later that morning. Instead of falling into bed and sleeping her Saturday away, she'd called as soon as the shop opened and made an appointment. She wasn't in dire need of a trim, but she desperately needed to put out her own version of last night's events so rumors didn't get totally out of hand.

Lester Boggs had been a braggart in high school; Amy had no reason to think he'd reformed in the eleven years she'd been away from town. He'd waste no time passing along the news that she'd come in at dawn with Grayson Phillips.

Sleepy and anxious, she took a lesson from Gray and pasted a convincing smile on her face as she pushed open the wood door with a single diamond glass pane and walked inside. The smell of perming solution hit her so hard she blinked tears from her eyes. The salon she'd used in Fort Worth had better ventilation, but certainly not as reliable a system of gossip.

"Good morning, ladies," she said cheerfully as she peeled off her jacket and threw it over one of the aqua-and-chrome chairs.

"Well, good morning," Joyce said, looking up from her appointment, an older lady Amy didn't recognize. "I'll be finished in just a moment."

Amy waved her hand. "No problem. I have all day." She looked around the beauty shop, which in no way could be called a styling salon. Joyce hadn't updated her furnishings or her hair color in a quarter century, not that anyone in town was complaining. Everyone liked the beautician just the way she was—meddling and all.

Olive, who tended bar nights at Schultze's Roadhouse, looked up from her magazine, two-dozen pink perming rods bobbing with the movement. "Even after that late night?" she asked with a touch of humor in her husky voice.

"We did have a wonderful time at the fundraiser," Amy said cheerfully. "It's always nice to support a good cause."

"Or spend time with a good-looking man," Olive added.

"Watch out," Joyce warned. "I think Olive's jealous that she's too old to catch Grayson Phillips's attention."

"Hmm," the permed bartender replied, going back to *True Confessions.*

"Still," Joyce said, giving the older lady in the chair a final spritz of hair spray, "you must have had a good time. I heard you really made a night of it."

"You know," Amy said, looking casually through the magazines stacked on the beige Formica end table, "that banquet food was pretty bad. We ended up going out for something later and just got to talking. You know how time slips by."

"When you're having fun," Olive finished.

"Yes, that too." Amy pretended to study a recent edition of *Good Housekeeping.* "Not that either one of us is looking for anything serious. I mean, we'll probably see each other around town, but I doubt we'll make a repeat of last evening.'' Which is just what he'd told her—only in more definitive terms. Just what she'd agreed would be in their best interests.

''What a pity,'' Joyce said, tucking her customer's check inside one of the many drawers at her workstation. ''I'll bet you two made a very attractive couple.''

Amy shrugged. ''Gray's a real gentleman, but I got the impression he's very dedicated to his business.''

''You know what they say about all work and no play,'' Olive warned from over the dog-eared top of *True Confessions*.

''I wouldn't worry. I'm sure he'll have plenty of dates in the future. There must be a few young ladies who haven't gone out with him.''

Even as she made the glib comment, she felt a pang in the area of her heart. Gray would have other dates, even if he no longer participated in the Ranger Springs version of ''The Dating Game.'' But she wouldn't be one of them.

ON MONDAY MORNING, the Wheatley Medical Clinic opened for the first time with a new doctor wearing a white coat. Her dad had surprised her with the gift as she arrived that morning. Tears had filled her eyes as she traced the embroidered script: ''Dr. Amy Wheatley'' above ''Wheatley Medical Clinic.'' She'd owned other lab coats, but none given to her by her gruff-but-loving Daddy. None delivered with a strong hug and words of praise from father to daughter.

As Gladys Metzier, their nurse and receptionist, unlocked the door, Amy felt more nervous flutters than she had during her residency. After all, these were her neighbors, former classmates and teachers, and friends. There would be new faces—people who'd moved to the area and children that had been born—but she'd still know most of her patients by name.

Her father was around for consultations, although Amy thought he spent most of his time reading the newspaper and chatting with Gladys. She'd been with her dad for about nine years, after his previous nurse had retired. Gladys knew everyone who came in, maintained all the records and ordered all their supplies. Amy was eternally grateful to have such a dependable helper.

Patients weren't filling up the seats of the waiting room. Perhaps word hadn't gotten out yet that the clinic was open, or maybe this was just a slow time. With the usual spat of colds and flu, Amy had anticipated more patients. Her father had kept reduced hours since his fall, often closing early when he couldn't bear his weight on his ankle any longer.

Her eleven o'clock appointment, Wanda Gresham, arrived a few minutes early. However, when Amy entered the exam room, the woman didn't appear all that eager to see the doctor.

"We've been coming to your father for years," the woman announced. "He doesn't seem too old to practice medicine."

Amy smiled. She understood patients' fears over seeing an unknown doctor. "He's still recovering from his fall, and being on his feet for a long time is difficult. I hope you'll give me a chance to show that I'm equally qualified to provide care for you and your family."

Mrs. Gresham harrumphed. There was no other description of the sound. "I hope your father is going to be around for a while. My husband is being treated for high blood pressure and poor circulation."

"I'll be glad to continue your husband's care, Mrs. Gresham. Does he have an appointment?"

"Not yet. I wanted to come in and meet you first."

So, perhaps Mrs. Gresham's unspecified knee joint pain wasn't as acute as she'd led Gladys to believe. Amy smiled in a reassuring manner. "I'll look forward to meeting Mr. Gresham when he comes in for his checkup."

The woman narrowed her eyes. "You are single, aren't you?"

"Yes, I am."

"You're also very young."

"Almost thirty. I believe I went to school with one of your sons."

Mrs. Gresham harrumphed again. "I'd feel a lot more comfortable if your father could continue to see my husband."

Amy found her reassuring smile harder to maintain. "I'll consult with my father, of course, but I'll do my best to provide good medical care for you and your family."

The negative remarks stayed with her long after the exam ended and her patient departed, though. She'd expected resistance, but for a patient to bring up her age *and* unmarried status… Well, she simply hadn't expected both those concerns.

What effect could her marital situation have on her patients? She decided to seek Gladys's advice. The woman knew every one of their patients in detail, far more than charts would indicate.

"Mrs. Gresham is convinced every woman she sees is out to steal her husband away from her," the nurse advised.

"Does he have a roving eye?" Not to mention roving hands, which Amy had also encountered in her practice among certain uncivilized individuals.

"Are you kidding? Mr. Gresham is kept on a pretty tight leash. I don't know what he did when he was younger, but ever since I've known them, he hasn't strayed."

"Then why is his wife so convinced he's going to look at other women."

Gladys shrugged. "Who knows? All I can say is be careful. That man needs medical treatment. He's a prime candidate for a stroke."

"Thanks, Gladys." Amy sighed and walked toward her dad's office—which was her office now, too. She was still having trouble thinking of the clinic and the desk as also her domain.

A blast of cold, fresh air swirled through the waiting room as Ambrose Wheatley hobbled inside.

"Good morning, ladies," he greeted for the second time that day. He'd left before the clinic opened to run an errand. Amy suspected he'd treated himself to a sweet roll and coffee at the café.

"Hi, Daddy," Amy said, trying to make her voice and expression cheerful.

"What's wrong, Amy girl? Not an emergency?"

"No, just one Mrs. Gresham who thinks I'm too young and unattached to treat her husband."

Her dad shook his head. "She'll come around. Some of these people just need a little time."

Time. Well, now that she was back in town to stay, Amy suspected she'd have plenty of that commodity. Especially since she wouldn't be going out on any more dates with Grayson Phillips.

AMY HAD DECIDED TO take Wednesday afternoons off so she had some free time during the week to conduct personal business or just spend some time away from the clinic. She hadn't had much time to start any hobbies in Forth Worth. Maybe now that she'd settled down, she could pursue some of her other interests. She'd love to look up some of her old friends, although she knew many of them had married and moved away. Looking up friends hardly qualified as a hobby.

First, she needed to find something interesting besides medicine. Immediately, Gray's image popped into her head. Now there was a man who could become a full-time hobby.

She shook off the unproductive thoughts as she pushed open the door of the Four Square Café. She had a craving for one of their turkey club sandwiches and French fries. Thelma and Joyce were just getting up from their usual chairs when Amy walked past to take a seat.

"Good afternoon, ladies."

"Amy! How nice to see you," Thelma greeted. The newspaper owner and editor had been nice enough to run an article on Amy's return to town and work at the clinic.

Joyce reached out and fluffed her hair. "How's that new cut coming?"

"Fine. I've gotten used to the layering around my face and I really like it."

"Good. It makes you look a little older. More sophisticated," Joyce added.

"I wish you'd convince some of my patients that I'm plenty old to practice medicine."

"Oh, they'll come around."

"That's what my father says, but I'm worried. I've had two women this week who hinted they didn't want their husbands treated by a young, single doctor."

"Old habits, my dear," Thelma answered. "Some of these people are very entrenched in their thinking."

"I'm just concerned. I'm sure things will work out."

"Of course they will," Joyce advised.

"Have you heard from our Mr. Phillips?" Thelma asked.

"No, I haven't." And she hadn't expected to, either. Not that she hadn't remembered him every night as she'd slipped between the cool sheets of her lonely bed.

"I thought perhaps he might have asked you out again."

"No. Why did you think so?"

"Because we mentioned a certain other young lady who needed a date for a wonderful arts event in San Marcus, and he claimed he was unavailable. For

Saturday night! Can't imagine why unless he had a previous engagement,'' the editor said, her expression questioning.

Amy shrugged. ''Not with me.'' But perhaps she knew why. Perhaps Gray had gotten tired of the constant demand for blind dates. Maybe after talking it though on their date, he'd decided to take a stand against the two matchmakers.

''We'll have to check back with him.''

''Maybe he just doesn't want to date,'' Amy suggested.

''Nonsense.''

''What if he *isn't* looking? Maybe he's happy being single.'' The idea of Gray with another woman caused a different type of pain near her heart. She wouldn't call it jealousy, because she had no claim upon his time or affections. But she did recognize the potential for problems. She absolutely couldn't start thinking about ''what ifs'' where Gray was concerned.

''Nonsense,'' Joyce said. ''Men just think they're happy single. It's up to women to convince them otherwise.''

Amy smiled and shook her head at their obvious rigid thinking on the subject of single men. ''Well, good luck, ladies. I've had my one date with Grayson Phillips.''

The two older ladies jerked to attention. ''One date? What do you mean by that?'' Thelma asked.

Oops. Amy knew she'd slipped up. She was certain Gray didn't want anyone else to know his unwritten rule of dating. She wasn't about to give away his secrets. ''I meant that I don't think he'll ask me out again. We had a good time, but I don't have any more events to attend in the near future. And surely he's a very busy man.''

Thelma narrowed her eyes in thought, and Joyce appeared to be scheming. Before they could come up with more questions, Amy hurried to an empty table.

ON FRIDAY AFTERNOON, two men showed up without an appointment. One worked at Grayson Industries; the other was the boss.

Amy had to take a few seconds to school her features and lower her pulse before she approached them. She hadn't seen Gray since she'd bolted from his car early Saturday morning. She'd even tried telling herself, in the dark hours of the night, that he wasn't as appealing as she'd remembered. She'd been wrong. His black knit shirt defined his impressive chest and accented his flat stomach and lean hips. A leather aviator-style jacket was thrown casually across one of the reception area chairs.

''Gray?'' Amy asked as she walked past the half-walled reception area. ''What are you doing here? Are you ill?'' He certainly didn't appear to be ailing. He looked…wonderful.

''No,'' he said, his gaze taking in every detail from her newly trimmed hair to her slightly rumpled lab coat. ''I brought one of my employees, Steve Curtis. He slipped while lifting a box and hurt his back.''

Thankfully, her father wasn't here at the moment to see his daughter stumble through this seemingly innocent meeting. Amy motioned for Gladys to come over.

''Would you take our patient into Exam One and

get him a gown?'' With a startled look, Steve followed Gladys out of the waiting room.

Of course, Amy realized a moment later, she was now alone with Gray. Had that been her subconscious intention? She wanted to say no, but how could she when the attraction was as strong as ever?

''Well, I'd better take a look at him. Umm, as soon as he's had a chance to get into the gown.'' She paused, her eyes hungry from the sight of Gray. He was dressed in business casual, but he looked even better than he had in a tuxedo. ''Will you stay?'' she asked, her voice sounding breathless and not at all professional, ''So I can give you an update on his condition?''

''I'll be here.'' His gaze told her he'd be waiting impatiently.

Her pulse started racing again and she felt her cheeks heat with a blush. She nodded in response, embarrassed by her reaction, unwilling to trust her voice. She should have been thinking of her patient, but all that she could remember for one moment was how Gray's kiss had sent her running for safety.

Resisting the urge to run once again, she grasped her stethoscope and hurried to her patient. After a knock on the closed door, she took a calming breath and stepped inside.

The young man in her exam room had changed into a gown, and was sitting on the padded table. Amy went through a series of questions and had him carefully move so she could determine the extent of his injury. She soon realized Steve wasn't in extreme pain, as she'd sometimes seen from lifting accidents.

Oh, there was discomfort, but hardly an emergency situation requiring immediate care.

She also discovered he was a bit amazed that the boss had taken him to the doctor, instead of advising the young man to drive himself to the clinic after work.

Interesting.

Either Gray was the most considerate, concerned boss she'd ever encountered, or he had another reason for coming to the clinic. Like seeing her, perhaps?

Interesting.

She wrote a prescription for painkillers, advised Steve not to drive while taking the medicine and told him to schedule a follow-up visit for next week.

Then she went back to the waiting room to find out why Gray had taken such a personal interest in his employee. Or if there might be another reason he was pacing the room instead of running his successful business.

Chapter Four

Gray shifted impatiently on the outdated chairs in the clinic's waiting room. How long did it take to look at one slightly strained back? More importantly, how long would Amy be cloistered in the exam room with the young, muscular stock room employee?

Gray inwardly cursed himself for a fool. He hadn't needed to bring Steve in for a checkup. Grayson Industries had plenty of supervisors and other employees who could have done the job. But as soon as he'd heard the thump of the fallen box, he'd interfered, thinking only of the excuse the injury would provide. An excuse to see Amy again.

She looked wonderful. Oh, not as polished and primped as she'd appeared on Friday night. Today she appeared more...wholesome. Very professional in her lab coat with her name embroidered above the name of the clinic. With her dark, glossy hair framing a face almost devoid of cosmetics.

Damn, but he still wanted her. He envied Steve who was "allowed" time with Amy. Who was allowed to removed his clothes for the doctor....

His slacks were too tight. The chair was too hard.

Gray couldn't get comfortable, and silently acknowledged that he might never be comfortable again. Not as long as Amy was so near, yet so out of reach.

He pushed out of the chair, needing to take some action while Steve—nearly naked with Amy just beyond that closed door—was examined. Pacing the room wasn't as satisfying as bursting into the exam room and hauling Amy into his arms.

Before he'd made his second trip across the linoleum, Amy exited the exam room, a thoughtful expression on her face. Gray ignored the receptionist and intercepted the doctor. ''Well?''

She met his gaze squarely, a slight question in her eyes. ''He'll be fine. I suggest light duty, such as no lifting over twenty pounds and no repetitive bending or stooping for another week.''

''I'll tell his supervisor.''

''Ah, yes. He does have an immediate supervisor, doesn't he?''

''Yes,'' Gray answered, confused by her knowing tone. ''Why do you ask?''

Instead of answering, she took his arm and led him into a corner office. A few empty boxes were stacked near the door, and her framed diplomas and licenses leaned against another wall.

After she closed the door, she said, ''I was just wondering if you take such a personal interest in all your employees.''

''What do you mean?'' He was having trouble keeping his mind on the conversation with her so close. Within touching distance. Within kissing range.

''Why did you bring Steve to the clinic, Gray?''

"Because he was injured."

"Not very seriously. Tell me, do you always personally escort your employees to the clinic?"

"We don't have that many injuries, but no, I don't."

Amy picked up a pencil holder, stared at the caduceus on the side, then placed it back on her desk. She looked up at him. "Did you want to see me, Gray?"

"Yes."

"Why?"

How could he respond to that direct question when he didn't know the answer. "I don't know, Amy."

"Then why here? You could have called me. We could have met somewhere else."

"You mean like your house...or mine?"

A slight blush stained her cheeks. "Or someplace else."

"I told you I didn't date anyone twice."

"So you found an excuse to bring your employee to the clinic."

"You make me sound devious."

Amy sighed. "Not devious, but not exactly honest either. I don't want to play games, Gray."

"You think I do? Believe me, I'm not proud of myself for acting like a..." He couldn't think of any word or phrase other than "love-struck fool" to describe what he was feeling.

"Gray—"

"I'm sorry, Amy. I'm not trying to play games. I just wanted to see you again."

She slumped against the desk. "Oh, Gray, I wanted to see you, too. But you made yourself clear, so I didn't call. I told everyone who asked that we probably wouldn't be going out again. I did what was necessary to honor your request."

He took a step closer and placed his hands lightly on her shoulders. "I appreciate that. What I said when we went out was the truth. Maybe this irrational urge I have to see you is all the more reason for staying away."

She tilted her head. "What do you mean?"

"Obviously, the attraction we both feel is strong. Unless you're willing to have a clandestine affair, I can't see any future for us."

"You really don't want to know how things might develop between us?" she asked, her voice soft and searching.

"Of course I want to know. Dammit, I go to bed aching for you. Believe me, that's not a normal situation for me. Not at this point in my life. But I was serious about my intentions—I don't want a long-term relationship. My company is my life, at least for now."

"So basically you'd like to have sex, but that's all."

Now he was the one blushing. Put that way, his words sounded crass, insensitive. The tension in her shoulders revealed her reaction to his admission. "I respect you too much to suggest we have a quick tumble on your couch, Amy. I'm just pointing out that people will be watching us. I would never do anything to jeopardize your standing in the community."

"I appreciate that, Gray," she said, her eyes focused somewhere around the baseboard. "But *I'm* just pointing out that you're sending mixed messages. How am I supposed to respond when you make excuses to come to my clinic, but claim we have no future?''

''Maybe just one time, like this,'' he said as he tipped her chin up and lowered his lips to hers.

AMY ALLOWED HERSELF A moment to respond. Or perhaps ''allow'' was too strong a word. How could she stop her breath from catching, her heart from racing, or her lips from melting into his? Just for a moment. He tasted of cinnamon and forbidden longings. He very nearly took away her will to resist, and all the good sense she'd been raised with. Amy might have lived in the ''big city'' for the past eleven years, but she wasn't going to toss aside all her scruples for one or two nights of mind-blowing passion. Even for Grayson Phillips.

She pulled away, her mind spinning, her lips swollen. ''You have to leave now.''

''I can't leave now,'' he said, resting his forehead against hers. ''If I do, your nurse and my employee will know what we've doing in here.''

The bulge in his trousers pressed against her stomach. Oh, yes. She didn't need a medical degree to know what *that* meant. ''If you don't leave, we might be doing more than kissing.''

Gray closed his eyes and groaned. ''Don't say things like that.''

Amy dug her nails out of his back and pulled her hands around to his chest. ''Gray, this is crazy. To quote a cliché, 'we can't keep meeting like this.'''

''You're right,'' he said, smoothing a wispy strand

of hair back from her cheek, "but I'm not one hundred percent sure I can stay away."

"I can't play this game."

"It's not a game."

"It's not real, either. What would you call it?"

He closed his eyes, took a deep breath and shook his head. When he looked at her again, his silvery eyes reflected her confusion. "I don't know. Maybe we both met at a…vulnerable moment. You'd just moved back to your hometown, I'd been out of a relationship for a long time…"

"Sounds rational. Do you believe it?"

"I have to believe something sensible."

"Then believe this—I won't keep seeing you in private and pretend there's nothing between us. Either we date openly, get to know each other better or we stay away from temptation."

"Is that your final answer?"

Despite the serious discussion, Amy had to smile. "Yes, it is." She pushed away from him, fluffed her hair back into some semblance of normalcy, and straightened her lab coat. Thank goodness she didn't wear lipstick during office hours; it would have been all over her face. "I'm going to check with Gladys on your employee's follow-up appointment. You have about two minutes to appear in the waiting room."

Gray nodded. "Thanks."

She walked to the door, but paused before turning the knob. "Gray, I mean it. This attraction we have for each other…it's a little overwhelming. I have a lot going on in my life at the moment. I'm not good at lying; I always got caught when I tried."

"I understand. I don't want to put you in a situation where you'd have to deny anything."

She took one last look at his well-toned body, just-kissed lips and sex-starved eyes before slipping out the door. She'd said everything that needed to be said. Whatever decision Gray made about exploring a possible relationship—or not—she'd live with.

Or so she thought…until she nearly ran into her father, just outside her office door.

"Daddy! What are you doing here?"

"Last time I checked, I still worked here," he said, a little chuckle in his voice. "You look flummoxed, Amy girl. What's wrong?"

"Nothing, Daddy," she said, pushing some irritating wisps of hair behind her ear. "I'm finishing up for the day. I just saw a back injury." She looked over her father's shoulder. "There he is now. I'd better go check on his follow-up appointment."

She almost ran to Gladys's desk, hoping her father would take the hint and go into his own office. Or even stop for the day. If he left there might not be a problem. She wouldn't have to explain—"

"Gray!"

Oh, great. Amy turned around in time to see her father reach out to shake hands with the one man who didn't need to be in the clinic.

"Dr. Wheatley. How are you?"

"Fine, fine, son. What brings you to our clinic today? You're not the back injury Amy was mentionin', are you?"

Gray glanced at her across the ten feet or so separating them. "I brought my employee in to see Dr.

Wheatley,'' he said, then added with a smile, ''Dr. Amy Wheatley.''

Her father glanced between them, then back at her previously closed office door. She'd always thought the term ''the air was charged'' was just some dramatic overstatement. Now, as she looked from Gray to her father and imagined what her dad might be thinking, she knew the term was entirely accurate.

''Ah. I see,'' her father said.

''Mr. Phillips, I need you to sign this form,'' Gladys said, interrupting the uncomfortable tension. Thank goodness for Gladys.

Amy stepped out of the way. Gray had to walk past her to get to the reception desk. As he passed by, he gave a little shrug, as if he were saying, ''What can I do?''

She had no idea. When she glanced at her father, he was smiling. Bad news. He'd obviously made some big assumptions about what was going on between her and Gray.

Darn it, he'd probably come to some pretty accurate assumptions. She hadn't looked in the mirror, but she likely appeared as if she'd been thoroughly kissed.

''That's all we need for now. I'll file these forms, and send your company the invoice for whatever the insurance company doesn't pay,'' Amy heard Gladys explain to Gray.

''Thank you.'' He turned around, gave her a slight smile, and looked at her father. ''Dr. Wheatley, it was good to see you again. Amy...thank you for taking care of Steve.''

"You're welcome." She folded her arms beneath her breasts.

"Come back anytime," her father said cheerfully.

Gray nodded, then joined his employee in the waiting room. After grabbing his jacket, he exited the clinic. Amy exhaled.

"Well, well," her father said. "Looks like you and Gray hit it off real good the other night."

"Daddy, don't start," she warned, turning toward her office. As soon as she got to the doorway, however, she realized that was a bad idea. Too many memories lurked just inside. Warm, firm lips. A hard body. Seductive silver eyes.

She stopped and faced her father. "We had a nice chat, but like I told you before, there's nothing going on."

"Not yet, but you hang in there. I can tell he's interested."

"Daddy, it's not—"

"I've got to go, Amy. There's a piece of apple pie with my name on it down at the café."

Amy slumped against the doorway. Her father was firmly convinced his matchmaking was working. She hated to disappoint him, but sooner or later, he was going to learn she and Gray had no future.

NEXT WEDNESDAY ON Amy's afternoon off, she decided to treat herself to lunch at the Four Square Café. Surely most of the people who might be talking about her and Gray would have already eaten lunch. Not that she could avoid all gossip; she'd gotten an earful from both her father and Gladys. Both of them thought Gray was great, and couldn't imagine any reason he and Amy wouldn't be dating. She'd been unable to gently burst their bubbles, so she'd simply given up.

A few minutes before one o'clock, she pulled into a parking spot facing the small park at the center of the square. The weather had warmed considerably from the cold front two weeks ago. In the oak trees around a small center gazebo, a steady westerly breeze rattled dried, brown leaves. Squirrels scampered off, their cheeks bulging with acorns. Concrete planters of yellow chrysanthemums and hardy, orange marigolds lent color to the brown and gray of the winter landscape.

The old-fashioned bell over the door tinkled when she entered. Expecting to find the café mostly empty, she was startled to find a small crowd gathered around one of the red vinyl booths near the back. She identified Thelma and Joyce, Pastor Carl and one of the waitresses. Then the group parted, revealing Gray standing next to a booth where Gina Summers was seated.

Gina was the local real estate agent, but by the look on her face, Amy suspected the group wasn't discussing home prices in Ranger Springs. Gray didn't appear any happier. Instead of his normally calm expression, he wore one of near panic. Nevertheless, he looked great to her eyes, tall and proud and so handsome he took her breath away. Today he wore a long sleeve charcoal sweater that looked like cashmere, and pleated black slacks that fit him like they'd been woven to the exact specifications of his body.

But now was not the time to ogle Grayson Phillips.

Whatever was going on in that back booth, Amy didn't want any part of it, she thought as she slipped into a chair near the door. She might be as curious as the next person, but she knew when to leave people alone. The group gathered around Gina definitely looked like they were up to something.

"AMY," GRAY SAID AS HE stopped next to her table. "I need to talk to you."

She looked up, surprise mixing with welcome in her blue eyes. "Gray. I thought you were busy."

"That's what I need to talk to you about. Do you mind if I join you?"

"Please," she said, indicating the empty chair across from her.

He sat, then leaned forward. "Act as though you're glad to see me. Like you were expecting me." He smiled for the benefit of his audience, some fifteen or twenty feet away. "Could you do that for me, please?"

She leaned forward also, some unknown emotion flashing in her blue eyes. "Is this how you got into trouble at Gina Summer's booth?"

"No."

Amy leaned back, studying him. She shook her head, as if to clear her thoughts, then said, "I am glad to see you. I'm just a tad confused. This may be none of my business, but what's going on?"

"They're trying to fix me up with Gina for the Harvest Festival Dance at the church. She's handling the fund-raising booths, and my company is providing the entertainment. My personal dating team and the pastor feel it would be logical for me to attend with her. I like Gina, but I've already had one date with her."

"When?"

Gray shrugged. "I'm not sure. Maybe three months ago."

"And you don't want to reveal your one-date rule."

"Right."

"Gray, your rule is making your life more complicated than it needs to be."

He shook his head. Amy didn't understand. He couldn't show favoritism among the women he'd dated. He'd learned that in a small town, word got around quickly, especially when an eligible bachelor and an attractive, single woman were involved. He'd heard enough talk when his own marriage had ended so dramatically four years ago—and their breakup had occurred in Dallas.

"I can't let people believe Gina is the one woman in this entire area who warrants a second date from Grayson Phillips. What about all the other women I've never asked out again? And then, if I don't ask Gina out after the Harvest Dance, she'll be under scrutiny from Thelma, Joyce and who knows who else."

"My, you're pretty impressed with yourself, aren't you?" Amy said. Her words stung, but her tone sounded teasing. He looked into her eyes, but for once couldn't read her expression. Before he could decide how to respond, Thelma and Joyce arrived at the table.

Thelma spoke first. "Hello, you two. How are you, Amy?"

"Fine. And yourself?"

"Just peachy." The newspaper editor turned her attention from Amy to him. "Gray, have you made a decision about the festival? We think your attendance with a date would be great publicity. More ticket sales mean more good deeds," Thelma said.

"We appreciate all you've done already," Joyce added. "But I think Thelma and Pastor Carl are right."

Gray looked from the two older ladies to Amy. *Help me,* he wanted to beg. *Think of some brilliant reason I can't go out with Gina without revealing my one unbending rule of dating.* As he looked into her eyes, he sensed she'd read him mind, that she had come up with something utterly brilliant.

"Ladies, could you excuse us for a moment?" Amy asked. "I need to discuss something with Gray before he makes his decision."

"Of course," Thelma said, raising one eyebrow. She and Joyce shared a look that said "this got interesting."

Joyce said, "We'll just go visit with Pastor Carl while you two young people confer."

"Gray, let's take a walk," Amy said as soon as the two older ladies departed. Her blue eyes sparked with anticipation. "I have a suggestion."

She was going to suggest he drop his one-date rule—again, he thought as he held the door open for her. Well, he couldn't do that in good faith. Amy was going to have to accept his feelings about not putting others in an uncomfortable position. Besides, how, in good faith, could he ask another woman out for a date when all he wanted to do was pull Amy into his arms and kiss her until they were both breathless?

"I KNOW WHAT YOU'RE going to say," Gray said as they took a seat on a park bench across from the café. "My one-date rule is causing problems. Well, maybe, but dating randomly, without any thought to the feelings of others, would be equally wrong."

"You're right," Amy said, watching the surprised expression on Gray's face. "You've probably saved a dozen women from potential hurt."

"Then what...why did you want to take a walk?"

Amy leaned toward him, barely resisting the urge to squeeze his forearm or give him a shake, just to make sure she held his attention. "Because in saving all those women from a second date—and possible high expectations of a future relationship—you've caused problems for yourself that can no longer be ignored."

"Granted, I'm getting tired of fending off Thelma and Joyce's matchmaking, but perhaps, over time, I can persuade the ladies—"

Amy shook her head. "It'll never happen. They're determined and have unlimited resources—i.e. the town's approval and the power of word of mouth."

"Gossip," Gray clarified.

Amy shrugged. "Whatever you call it, you're only one man against many. I believe a different approach is needed."

"Like what? Should I start being rude to them? I don't think I can. They're so sweet, and deep down inside, they believe they have my best interests at heart."

"Well, as a physician, I say that all this matchmaking is causing too much stress. You have to take care of your mind and body." And what a body he had to care for, Amy silently added. She longed to run her hand over the hard muscles of his arms, encased in the soft weave of his sweater. She'd like to plough her fingers through his salt-and-pepper hair, then skim downward over his wide shoulders and strong back.

Was it suddenly ten degrees warmer in the park? Her navy blazer, white T-shirt and jeans suddenly seemed way too hot and itchy.

"So your interest is purely professional?" Gray asked, amusement in his voice. She could tell he didn't believe that to be the case.

"No, not entirely. We've already discussed this attraction we feel for each other. With you not dating the same woman twice, and me not interested in a clandestine affair—"

"Which I don't feel would be right, either," Gray added.

Amy nodded. "Understood. However, that leaves us both with the same problem—people who are trying to get us paired off. They know the right person is out there for us if we'd just go on enough dates to find them."

"So what do you propose?"

Propose. Now there was a loaded word if she ever heard one. Shaking aside doubts about the wisdom of her impromptu plan, she plunged ahead. "I think you and I should team up to thwart the matchmakers."

"Gee, do we get a secret decoder ring? Should I

build a clubhouse in the backyard?'' Gray joked, obviously not taking her seriously. ''Or maybe you'd like me to bug the café.''

''No, but we might want to sign a blood oath never to tell anyone our purpose. Seriously, Gray, listen to my plan.''

''I'm listening,'' he said, turning toward her with a slight smile ''I'm sorry, but so far you've made this sound like James Bond mission.''

She took a deep breath and watched a squirrel scamper up a nearby tree. The animal twitched its tail at her, taunting her as if it didn't give much credence to her idea, either. ''It's a little more personal. I don't take my happiness, or the happiness of my father, lightly.''

''What's your plan?'' Gray asked, brushing a strand of hair behind her ear.

His sudden caress startled her. Her skin tingled, and she resisted the urge to lean toward his warmth. Suddenly she wasn't sure her spur-of-the-moment plan would work. Not if she had to keep her hands off Gray, which she absolutely, positively must do. Taking a deep breath, she decided to plunge ahead anyway. He could always say no. They could discuss the pros and cons like rational adults.

As long as he kept his hands—and lips—to himself.

''Okay. I think we should pretend to be dating. Or maybe pretend is the wrong word. We would actually date, but with the express purpose of keeping our overzealous matchmakers at bay. They'd have to really believe us, of course. Whatever social functions you'd normally attend, I'd go with you. We'd need to be seen around town, at the Bretford House restaurant or maybe in Wimberley."

"Sort of a relationship of convenience," Gray said carefully.

"Right! Both of us would benefit. You'd get Thelma and Joyce off your back, and I'd make my father happy. He thinks very highly of you, and would love the idea of us being a couple."

"But what about in the long run? Wouldn't you be setting yourself up for more problems when our pretend relationship actually ended?"

Amy shrugged. "In time, we could have a friendly breakup. I'm sure my father would accept our explanation, especially if he believed we just weren't compatible in the long run."

Gray seemed to be pondering her proposal. His forehead creased and his lips thinned as he stared down at the frost-damaged grass. "What would you consider grounds for ending the relationship of convenience?"

"I hadn't thought that far ahead." The fact she was thinking of all the positives and none of the negatives should have alarmed her, but she felt uplifted and empowered. She and Gray would be doing something positive for everyone who cared for them. Plus, they'd get to spend time together, which would probably make them both happy…for a while, at least.

"What if you found someone else?" he asked.

"Or you did," she added, looking up into his eyes. "That sounds like good grounds to call it quits."

"What else?"

"If we tire of one another." Amy smiled. "If you find you can't spend another night in my company without strangling me, I'd certainly appreciate a heads up.''

Gray smiled. ''Done. And I'd expect the same.''

''So you agree?'' This seemed so easy! She'd expected she'd have to sell him on the idea a little more. Put up more arguments. Instead, he'd caved very quickly.

''I think your plan has a lot of potential,'' he said cautiously.

''Do you have reservations?''

Gray was silent a moment, looking into her eyes, making her forget if *she* had any qualms about such an agreement. ''I'm a cautious person by nature, but I also believe in instincts. My instincts say 'yes, go for it!' but I'd like to think about your idea for a few hours, maybe overnight.'' His eyes darkened to a stormy gray as he reached up and smoothed another errant strand of hair behind her ear. ''I'm not sure I can evaluate anything logically when you're around.''

''I know what you mean. To be honest, that's my only reservation.''

''What?'' he asked softly.

''That we won't be able to control this attraction we feel for each other.''

''Do we need to control it?''

Amy paused, closed her eyes for a moment, and then opened them so she could watch Gray's expression. Sexual awareness sparked between them as easily as summer lightning. ''I'm not sure there would be anything 'convenient' about taking our relationship from dating to something more...physical.''

"So," he said, his fingers tracing the line of her cheek, down to her jaw, then lower, "we keep our hands to ourselves."

"Maybe we need to set some guidelines," she said, her voice husky, breathless.

"Kissing, but nothing more?"

She'd counseled young girls about the dangers of getting "carried away" by passion with their equally immature boyfriends, but she'd never had to warn herself to act like a responsible adult. "Can we trust each other to stop with kisses?"

"I'm not sure," he said. Gray eased back on the bench. "That's one of the things I'd like to think about."

The November breeze cooled Amy's overheated cheeks. "You'll call me later?"

"Oh, yeah," he said, rising from the bench in one smooth move. He extended a hand and helped her up. "Now I'd better get inside and explain to Thelma and Joyce that I can't take Gina to the Harvest Festival dance. A certain brunette doctor might get jealous," he said with a twinkle in his silvery eyes.

He might be teasing, Amy thought as they walked back to the Four Square Café, but there was a lot of truth in that glib remark.

Chapter Five

Could he keep his hands off her if they spent a lot of time together? Gray wondered. He couldn't get Amy's unexpected, yet surprisingly simple, proposal out of his mind after he returned to his office. Did he even want to try? He supposed she was right; they should confine their physical contact to whatever they could control, because all the reasons not to get involved still existed. He wasn't looking for a relationship; she didn't want an affair. They had their reputations to consider. They both had futures in this town, and his didn't include falling for and marrying the town doctor, who was loved like a daughter by most of the Ranger Springs residents. If the relationship didn't work out, if he somehow screwed up, he could barely imagine the repercussions to his reputation and company.

As for Amy, she deserved a devoted husband, someone who would be supportive of her practice and a good father to their children. Gray knew he didn't fit the bill. He might remarry some day, but to a woman who would be an asset to his business, who understood the long hours he sometimes spent at work and who wouldn't put emotional demands on him. He didn't want the feeling of being "tied down" in a marriage.

But did he want to be tied into a relationship of convenience with Amy? Would he feel encumbered by their public appearances and private moments? His gut reaction said no. Amy wasn't like most women he'd dated since the divorce, probably because she also wasn't looking for a husband at the moment. Or maybe she was simply easier to be around, to talk to, than other women. He wasn't sure, because he'd never given his other dates a chance to get beyond the awkward first contact, when both people were trying hard to make a good first impression.

Maybe that was the difference, he thought as he walked out of the Grayson Industries offices toward his car. At first he'd stuck to his "date face," keeping his remarks polite and polished. But he hadn't been able to maintain that persona for long with Amy. Somehow, she drew him out of his aloof behavior and into his natural personality. He'd taken her to his cabin on Lake Buchanan, he'd shared his dating secret with her, and he'd kissed her as a man kisses a woman he desires, not as a polite date kisses someone goodbye.

He eased the Lexus out of the parking lot and onto the farm-to-market road that wound its way through rocky hills covered in mesquite and other stunted trees to his home. Could he keep his hands to himself and his mind off making love to Dr. Amy Wheatley? Perhaps. Then again, he thought with a smile, maybe the good doctor wouldn't be able to keep her hands off him. An interesting complication, one he could live with.

He firmly believed there was a big difference between physical desire and emotional commitment. If Amy felt the same way, they might enjoy more than occasional dates. If she didn't...well, then they could still have a good time together.

His mind made up, he decided to call her as soon as he got home. His heart felt lighter as he imagined the weeks and months to come, with no further blind dates, with a beautiful, intelligent woman at his side.

Yes, the future was definitely looking up.

THE HARVEST FESTIVAL AT the church was always scheduled the weekend before Thanksgiving, putting everyone in the mood for the holiday season. Amy had been to the festival dozens of times in her life, but never as an adult with a date. A date who produced more attention than a two-headed calf at a carnival. A date who made her feel both special and nervous at the same time.

She and Gray strolled side by side, not holding hands or linked arm and arm, through crowds consisting of her friends and neighbors. An occasional group of children ran through the festival attendees, their high-pitched squeals as common as the taped organ music coming from the kiddie rides in the back parking lot.

She smiled and nodded at Ralph Biggerstaff, the Ranger Springs banker who was a long-time patient of her father. His persistent bursitis must not be acting up today, since he was walking around saying hello to bank patrons.

Surprisingly, Gray knew most of the people they encountered. He must have attended many social events in the months he'd lived in Ranger Springs, while she was still in Fort Worth. Occasionally she stopped to introduce him to a farmer or rancher who didn't spend much time in town. She wasn't sure he wanted to know everyone within a fifty-mile radius, but as far as she was concerned, the more people who knew they were a couple, the better.

"Thanks for coming to the festival with me," she said as they walked slowly past a booth offering popcorn and soft drinks. "I forgot how much I missed this annual event. Most of the time, I came with a group of friends."

"Not dates?"

She shook her head. "Not usually, although when I was a junior in high school, I accomplished the near impossible and got a date with the quarterback from Wimberley. He was a bit of a local hero, and I was feeling awfully good about myself that day." She ended with a laugh, remembering the teenage pressures to both conform and excel.

"Why do you say it was the 'near impossible?' I would imagine you could have dated anyone you wanted to."

"Thanks for the vote of confidence, but I was up against some pretty steep competition. Lots of girls from Wimberley, plus all the other small towns around here. Believe me, even without his athletic ability, Jason had his pick of dates."

"A real jock, hmm?"

"Yes, and I thought I'd reeled him in until..."

"What?"

"Oh, this sounds so childish now, but you remember Maryanne Bridges from the charity event in Austin?" At Gray's nod, Amy continued. "Just when I thought I'd be going steady with Jason, she decided she wanted him."

"And whatever Maryanne wants, she gets, I take it?"

"Right." Amy shook her head. Without thinking, she looped her arm through Gray's. "I was so angry with her...well, let's just say that it's a good thing my skills didn't extend to archery. Maryanne might still have an arrow sticking out of her—never mind."

Gray laughed. "I think I get the picture." He caressed her hand, then snuggled her close against him. He stopped in front of a booth offering games of skill, according to the sign. "Would you like a stuffed animal? I'm not sure my aim is as accurate as old Jason the quarterback, but I'll give it my best shot."

Amy laughed, thoroughly enjoying the Indian summer day, the familiar smells of popcorn and taffy and sounds of children laughing. And especially the man beside her. "I'd love for you to win a stuffed animal for me. Big or small, I'm not picky."

She hadn't been telling the truth, she realized a moment later as Gray paid for three baseballs and sized up the game. She was picky, but only when it came to the men in her life. She wouldn't have proposed this pretend dating situation with anyone else.

Fifteen minutes later, a bright purple teddy bear clasped in one arm and Gray in the other, Amy spotted two of the people responsible for this situation.

When she realized they were also arm in arm, she stumbled.

"Are you okay?" Gray asked as she regained her balance on the flat, dry lawn beside the church.

"Am I hallucinating, or is that my father with Joyce?"

Gray turned his attention to the crowd, finally spotting her dad. "That's what I'm seeing too. I didn't know your father was involved with Joyce."

"I didn't either," Amy answered, wondering how she really felt about her dad with another woman. Her heart had sped up, her mind going blank for just an instant when she'd first seen them. She was surprised, but not offended. Her father deserved a personal life. Her mother had been gone for nearly eighteen years, and to the best of Amy's knowledge, her dad had never been involved with another woman.

Maybe now that she'd returned to Ranger Springs, Amy thought, he finally had time to pursue a romantic relationship. Why not with Joyce? The beauty shop owner was attractive, perky and smart. Had her father just noticed those facts, or had he dated Joyce before and kept their relationship a secret?

Don't be ridiculous, Amy told herself. There were no secrets in a small town. *Not unless the two people conspired together to deceive everyone,* she reminded herself. She and Gray were doing a good job so far, but she didn't believe either her father or Joyce had the type of personalities that could keep such a secret for long.

Guilt at deceiving her father surfaced, this time more persistent because she was publicly admitting her relationship to Gray. She didn't like the feeling of guilt, but after seeing the look of delight on Ambrose Wheatley's face when she'd announced their date for the Harvest Festival, how could she tell him this was all pretend? Perhaps someday she'd be forced to reveal the deception, but until then, she appreciated his enjoyment in what he considered a great coup d'état—getting her "fixed up" with the town's most eligible bachelor.

"I think they just saw us," Gray said.

"Then we'd better smile and greet them. My father is tickled pink that we're 'dating.' I wouldn't want to shatter the illusion." Sure enough, her dad nodded in their direction and guided Joyce toward them.

"Just be yourself. I don't think there's any way we'll give away our secret, not if we're truly enjoying each other's company."

"I'm having a good time," she said, giving Gray's muscular forearm a small squeeze to emphasize her point.

"I am too," Gray replied, smiling down at her, his silvery eyes sparkling with interest and perhaps a bit of mischief. "Let's say hello to those two matchmakers. Maybe we can give them back a little of their own medicine."

Amy laughed, then she and Gray were standing before her father and Joyce. Amy pushed aside her guilt and joined in the fun of watching Dr. Ambrose Wheatley squirm under personal questions that skirted but never crossed the bounds of date etiquette. After all, she'd learned from some of the best—her dad and the rest of the town—and the turnabout *was* fair play.

OVER THE NEXT TWO WEEKS, Amy established a normal routine. Office hours, paperwork and Wednesday afternoons off. Sunday morning at church with her dad, Friday night dates with Gray.

And sometimes, she recalled as she dropped a used tongue depressor into the medical waste bin, Saturday afternoons with him as well.

"All done," she said to the young man who came in with symptoms of sore throat and chest congestion. He'd removed his flannel shirt so she could listen to his lungs. She seemed to be seeing more young men lately than she would have expected, and sometimes for illnesses or conditions most men didn't seek medical attention.

She wondered briefly if the fact she was young and single had anything to do with her patient mix, but then dismissed the idea. She couldn't imagine men making appointments just to see her…but then, she had a hard time believing insecure wives would keep their husbands away from critically needed medical care. Mr. Gresham hadn't made an appointment to have his blood pressure checked. She'd have Gladys follow-up.

"Get dressed and I'll write out a prescription for antibiotics and a decongestant."

"Thanks, Doctor."

Amy closed the door to the exam room and headed for her office. As usual lately, when she wasn't examining a patient or updating their records—and sometimes even when she was—her thoughts turned to Gray.

They'd eaten dinner at Bretford House last week and a German restaurant in Wimberley the weekend before to establish them more firmly as a couple. Amy had made sure the regulars at the café knew about the dates, just in case her father failed to mention the situation. Not that his silence was at all likely, Amy thought wryly.

But then Gray had invited her to go to San Antonio this Saturday afternoon to pick up a piece of art he'd purchased and had framed at a gallery. They wouldn't be seeing any people from Ranger Springs, so the invitation had nothing to do with their pretend relationship.

He'd asked her because he wanted to be with her. The idea was exciting, yet frightening. As long as the relationship was one of mutual convenience with established rules, she could handle the attraction she felt for Gray. Outside the boundaries of their pretend dating, she felt too much. Too tempted by his charm and good looks, too fascinated by his complex personality. She wanted to know why he presented such a controlled presence to the world, yet could act impulsively and with such strong passion while in private.

If they stepped outside the bounds of their relationship, how could she control her reaction to Gray? How much did she want to try to stop this attraction?

Should she go with Gray to San Antonio? She stepped inside her office, her eyes focusing on the purple teddy bear she'd sat on the shelves across from her desk. Gray had spent nearly twenty dollars winning the small stuffed animal, but hadn't seemed to mind. He'd been more amused than irritated by his inability to hit the target. Amy loved the fact he wasn't overly competitive. She'd grown up around boys who gloried in the rodeo, who spent all their money on customizing pickup trucks and who grew into men who boasted about being the best at anything and everything. Some doctors were so competitive and insecure that she found their boasting laughable. She'd never found that trait attractive.

What about *her* competitive tendencies? The need to confront and win only came out around Maryanne Perkins Bridges. Amy didn't like the feeling, and she didn't like admitting her weakness. Something from her childhood, some basic insecurity, surfaced around her old nemesis.

But the heck with Maryanne! Amy had more pressing problems at the moment, like deciding what to do about Gray's request. Should she go to San Antonio with him? Well, she did have a little more Christmas shopping to do. Perhaps they could stop at one of the malls. Maybe have an early dinner before—

"Are you about finished with that prescription?" the nurse interrupted her thoughts in a peeved tone. "Your patient is twiddling his thumbs."

Amy turned to Gladys. "Sorry. I'll bring it out in just a second."

Darn it, she'd done it again. Her thoughts had strayed to Gray when she should be focusing on her patients. What was it going to take to get her mind off their pretend dating and back to reality?

THE GALLERY WAS LOCATED near downtown, which teemed with tourists and shoppers just two weeks before Christmas. Gray found a parking spot in a lot nearby and they walked a block or so to the shop.

Amy hoped the art wasn't too large; carrying a heavy, framed piece back to the car would be awkward.

"You never did tell me what you purchased," she said as she pulled her jacket close. A cold front had turned the weather chilly, even this far south.

"It's hard to describe," Gray said. "A mixed media piece is what the gallery owner said."

"I don't know a lot about art."

"I don't either, but I needed something for the dining room."

"Didn't you have a decorator do your house?"

"Yes and no. You know my friend, Ethan Parker? He became chief of police while you were out of town. Well, his wife Robin is an interior decorator, and she helped a lot. I'm not into window treatments and the like, but she designed a minimalist approach I like. Many of the features are built in, so I worked with my architect."

"What's the style?"

"Kind of modern, I suppose, but using natural materials. I wanted it to blend into the hills."

"I imagine it's a lovely home."

Gray held the door to the gallery open for her. "I'd invite you to see it, but you might suspect my motives."

Amy smiled. "I might." She was pretty certain being alone with Gray in his isolated home wasn't a good idea. They had enough difficulty keeping their hands to themselves in a car or in her office with people nearby.

The transaction took very little time. Gray examined the art, which consisted of muted shades of burgundy, purple and teal watercolor and oil with a few gold leaf accents. The texture of various layers of paper gave interest to the abstract piece. The gallery owner had suggested a thin gold frame, which hid the canvas edges but didn't detract from the art.

Rather like Gray, Amy mused as she watched him. The packaging was nice—well-tailored clothes, touchable fabrics and heavenly scents—but the man himself was an original. Nothing in Gray's world detracted from his good looks and charm. She wondered how much of the "package" was contrived to give that effect and how much was a natural outgrowth of Gray's personality.

"And what does the lady think?" the gallery owner asked.

He obviously thought they were a couple. Perhaps even a married couple. An obvious error, and one she wasn't about to point out. There was no need to call attention to themselves here in San Antonio.

"I like it," Amy said as the dapper man held it up for her inspection.

"I do too," Gray said. "I wondered if I still would after several weeks, but I think it's going to look perfect in the dining room."

As the piece was carefully wrapped, Amy asked. "Do you entertain often?" Even though he was a businessman with contacts around the region, he was still single. She didn't believe he had a full-time housekeeper. At least, none of the gossips around the Four Square Café had mentioned anyone going to work for Gray in that capacity.

"No, but I intend to do more soon."

The gallery owner smiled. "If you'll pull around back, I'll have this loaded for you."

"Thank you," Gray said, taking Amy's arm and escorting her to the door. "Is there anything else you'd like to look at while we're here? You mentioned Christmas shopping, and Bertrauds has a good selection of gifts."

Amy doubted she could afford most of the items in the small shops along this street. Until the clinic adjusted to a high volume of patients, she was taking a cut in pay—not that she would ever mention that detail to Gray. Practicing medicine in Ranger Springs had never been about money. Just being with her dad was reward enough, she reminded herself.

"If it's okay with you, I'd rather stop by the mall on our way back to Ranger Springs. I'm familiar with the stores, and I have a list of the last few presents I need."

"Of course. I'm yours for the day," he said with a smile.

For the day. That's what they'd decided, after all. To take this pretend relationship one day at a time. To avoid long-term plans. She had to keep reminding herself of their agreement, especially on days like this, when they appeared to be a couple out shopping for artwork for their home and Christmas presents for their friends.

While the art was loaded into the trunk of the Lexus, Amy sat in the passenger seat and breathed in the familiar scents. She was reminded of their first date, and those since, when Gray had been so...gentlemanly. Since their agreement, he'd kept his word, avoiding situations where either one of them might be tempted. No more stolen kisses. No more lingering looks that melted her restraint. She appreciated his efforts, but sometimes, she wished—

The shrill buzz of her beeper jolted her back to reality. She fished the small device out of her purse. The clinic's number was followed by an emergency notification. Helen Kaminsky's grandson, Matthew, needed an emergency appendectomy.

She flung open the door after reading the rest of the message. "Gray! I've got to get to county hospital. One of my patients is there for an emergency procedure, and my father can't be reached." He'd probably forgotten his beeper again. He said he didn't like those "newfangled devices."

Gray slammed the trunk, his expression serious. "I'll get you there as quickly as possible. Do you have a cell phone?"

"No." She hadn't gotten a new one yet. The phone she'd used in Fort Worth had been provided by the practice.

"Use mine. Maybe you can find out more information."

"Thanks." She accepted the small, state-of-the-art device and entered the clinic's number as Gray steered the Lexus toward the interstate. Hopefully, Gladys was still answering the phone. If not, she'd call the hospital directly.

"I'm sorry to ruin your afternoon," she said to Gray as she counted the rings.

"No problem," he said, reaching over and grasping her hand. "I understand about work coming first."

Thankful for his understanding, Amy settled back

into her seat and watched the buildings of San Antonio pass by, along with other cars along Interstate 35 as they headed north. Gray was an excellent driver; she couldn't have gotten to the hospital any faster—unless, of course, she'd been in Ranger Springs instead of shopping in San Antonio.

But she wouldn't feel guilty for taking time off. Doctors had private lives, too. Helen's grandson would get excellent emergency care at the county hospital, Amy knew, until she could arrive in thirty-five to forty minutes.

As Gray followed her directions and pulled into the emergency entrance, she placed her hand on his arm. "Thank you so much. I'm sorry you got drafted to emergency service."

"Don't worry about it. Just go help your patient. I'll see you later."

"I'll get a ride home with Helen or someone."

Gray smiled, then leaned forward and brushed his lips over hers. The kiss was fleeting, so light she shouldn't have reacted strongly to the touch. But she did. Her pulse pounded hard and her breathing increased as she grasped the door handle.

"Go," Gray said, and she did, fleeing toward the hospital entrance and her waiting patient.

Chapter Six

As Gray settled into the molded plastic chair with a "fresh" cup of hospital coffee, he congratulated himself for his sterling behavior the past two weeks. As promised, he'd kept his hands—and other parts of his anatomy—to himself. Well, he silently corrected, except for that brief kiss this afternoon. Amy tempted him to forget the agreement, but when he looked into her clear blue eyes, he knew he couldn't disappoint her. She was depending on him to uphold his end of their deal, and he'd already pushed the bounds of their relationship by asking her to San Antonio for the afternoon.

He'd simply wanted to spend more time with her. He'd thought of little else during his leisure hours, with images of her face or snatches of her laughter drifting into his consciousness when he should have been concentrating on business. His preoccupation with Amy was a bad sign; he didn't want to become obsessed with the woman who was saving him from more blind dates. The problem was that he'd never had a similar relationship with another woman.

He wanted to call their bond a friendship, but he

wasn't sure if that was accurate. Did friends feel this mind-numbing attraction to each other? He'd had some female friends in college; he had female business associates with whom he was friendly. He'd never felt tempted to pull them into his arms and kiss them senseless.

Shifting on the hard seat, he wondered what she was doing now. She'd rushed into the emergency room, looking for the boy. He admired her dedication; he'd identified the same single-mindedness in himself. The difference was that his pursuit of new technology or additional business opportunities wasn't life or death. Amy's education and inclination toward medicine had given her the opportunity to save or significantly improve the lives of her patients.

Or maybe, he thought as he watched her walk down the hospital corridor toward the waiting room, her arm supporting the shoulders of a thin, worried woman, she sometimes made others feel better. Not because of medicine or healing, but because they trusted her knowledge and character. She might not be the surgeon who removed the boy's appendix, but she was the person the family wanted beside him when he was ailing. They trusted she'd see the right decisions were made in an environment foreign to most people.

He also trusted her, he realized. He couldn't say the same about too many people—just a few friends and a couple of business associates. He'd depended on himself for years, hiring the best employees and hoping they honored their confidentiality agreements. His high-tech products depended on getting a unique product to the market, which had been the U.S. government but was now expanding to include consumer products.

At one time, he'd trusted Connie. She'd been his wife, and before that, his college sweetheart. He'd loved her, but that hadn't been enough. His feelings hadn't compensated for the long hours and dedication to Grayson Industries. Her deception had been a total surprise. She'd never even hinted she wanted out of their marriage.

"How are you?"

He looked up into Amy's blue eyes. Realizing he was nearly crushing the cup of lukewarm coffee, he placed it carefully on the table and stood up. "I'm fine. Was that Mrs. Kaminsky you were with?"

"Yes. She headed for the pay phones to make a call." Amy ran a hand through her hair in a weary gesture. "You didn't have to wait for me."

"I didn't mind."

She frowned, her head cocked to one side. "You looked angry when I walked up."

Gray shook his head. "Not about you. I was thinking of something else. Something long past."

"You're sure?"

"Positive."

She stood in front of him, her gaze questioning. He knew she'd never push for details, but suddenly, he wanted to tell her something about his feelings.

"I was thinking of my ex-wife. She had an affair with my best friend. That's what I meant when I said the marriage was messy, not the divorce. She betrayed me, she wanted out but she didn't want a scandal. I gave her a small settlement, but she didn't get any part of my greatest asset, my business."

"I'm sorry you had to go through the divorce, though. The whole process must have been painful."

He shook his head. "I'm sure I was partially at fault. I was married to my company. Grayson Industries was my mistress, in a way. I suppose Connie believed she deserved the same level of attention from someone." He shrugged. "If it wasn't me, it would be someone else."

"Sounds sad for both of you."

"It's old news," he said, dismissing the conversation. He didn't want to talk about Connie, marriage, or divorce. He wrapped an arm around Amy's shoulders. "Are you finished with your patient?"

"Yes. Matthew came out of surgery just fine. His grandmother determined the symptoms were more serious than an upset stomach before the appendix ruptured."

"Good. Then how about I take you dinner? I'm starved."

"I'll bet you are," she said with a sympathetic smile. "Hospital coffee isn't the most tasty or nutritious snack."

"I'll agree. Let's see if we can find something more tasty and filling." In a place that had comfortable chairs and more subtle lighting.

And lots of people around so he didn't forget his dates with Amy were supposed to be for show, not for real.

AMBROSE WHEATLEY'S STEP felt a bit lighter as he headed for the Four Square Café and lunch with Thelma and Joyce. His broken ankle was mending nicely, but his heart soared beyond the restrictions of the walking cast or the cane he still had to use. Amy Jo's dates with Grayson Phillips were the best medicine he'd received in a month of Sundays. That young man was just what the doctor ordered—quite literally!

He chuckled at his own joke as he walked to Thelma and Joyce's table.

"You're in a good mood today," Joyce said, a glint of interest in her pretty green eyes.

"And why wouldn't I be?" he answered as he pulled out a chair next to the beautician and settled in for lunch. "I'm havin' a meal with my two favorite ladies, my daughter is datin' the most eligible bachelor in town and I'm feelin' fit as a fiddle."

"You won't be if you don't stay off that leg," Thelma reminded him.

"You sound just like my daughter," he complained.

"Oh, would that be your daughter, *the doctor?*"

Joyce giggled. "She got you on that one, Ambrose."

"I'm in too good a mood to let a little thing like a broken ankle bother me. Why, life is darn near perfect! Christmas is almost here, I might get me a son-in-law next year, and I'm enjoyin' the company of the prettiest lady in town—no offense, Thelma."

"None taken, Ambrose. I'm just glad your daughter didn't take as much time as you did to add some romance to her life."

"Are you callin' me a pokey old coot?"

"I never said a thing about you being an old coot."

Ambrose chuckled. "I don't hear any complaints

from the other side of the table,'' he said, looking at the lady he'd escorted around town for the past few weeks. Joyce was as cute as could be. As different from his dearly departed wife as night and day, but she'd been gone a good number of years. Talking to Amy had reminded him that it was about time he got on with his own life.

''What's the special for lunch today, ladies?'' he asked, reaching for a folded paper menu. His appetite for food and for life had jumped higher than a flea on a hound dog since his little girl moved back to town.

JUST A WEEK BEFORE Christmas, Amy sat on her black leather sofa and worried about how she was going to approach Gray regarding their relationship. Their supposedly *pretend* dating relationship. Since the emergency appendectomy, he'd behaved more like a real ''boyfriend'' than the man she'd conspired with to deceive the town.

She smoothed the pine green jersey dress over her legs, resisting the urge to pleat the soft fabric. She felt as fidgety as a three-year-old at Sunday church service, but she was determined neither Gray nor her father would know of her nervousness.

She should have kept the relationship uncomplicated by emotions. What was wrong with her? She had to focus or become forever lost somewhere between pretend and real, in a dimension with no past or future.

Except there was always a future. She'd learned that lesson as a child, when life had been going along so well. An idyllic community, two loving parents and lots of friends. Then one day everything had changed. Just one phone call and they'd rushed to the hospital. Not long afterward, her father had hugged her tight and told her that her mother was gone, the victim of a car accident. Gone, just like that. One minute Amy had been playing in her friend's yard in the warm sunshine; the next she'd been a child who would never see her mother again, or feel her strong, supportive hugs.

Oh, how she wanted life to stay constant. How she longed for the peace and contentment that came in the unchanging tempo of small-town life.

The sound of Gray's car in her driveway just before seven o'clock shook her out of the dark memories. They were due that evening at the community center for carols, punch, cookies and a visit with "Santa," also known as Dr. Ambrose Wheatley. The Christmas program provided lots of fun for children of all ages. She'd volunteered to keep the cookie trays stocked with all kinds of homemade goodies provided by ladies from the community.

As soon as she'd realized she was attending the program, she'd hesitated only a few minutes before calling Gray. First, her instincts had told her to tell him about the event, then ask him to escort her. Second, she wanted him beside her as the children crawled onto "Santa's" lap and told him their secrets. And last of all, she knew the merry matchmakers—as she and Gray had started called her father, Thelma and Joyce—would expect to see her there with Gray.

So tonight they would appear together in front of the town as a happy couple. Later, they needed to talk in private about the direction of their relationship. She was very concerned that both of them had forgotten *why* they were dating.

"YOU TWO TAKE A BREAK," Thelma ordered, taking the tin of cookies from Amy's hands. "Have some punch, get a breath of fresh air. Whatever you young people enjoy."

Gray smiled at the older woman's opinion that he was still a "young person." After a long day at the office, conference calls and an evening spent beside a beautiful woman he'd rather have all to himself, he didn't feel so young. He felt downright mature. Selfish, maybe, but hardly the type of carefree boy who could enjoy a Christmas party without thinking about how the green jersey hugged Amy's curves and set off her dark, shining hair.

A sprig of mistletoe over the entrance to the church's community center beckoned. He'd like to escort her to the bit of ribbon-bedecked greenery, take her in his arms and kiss her until the entire town knew how much he wanted her.

But that type of physical display would embarrass Amy, who needed to develop and maintain her professional reputation. She'd told him her medical practice had improved since they'd been dating, so at least one of her goals had been accomplished. He'd certainly enjoyed a respite from Thelma and Joyce's persistent efforts to get him matched with the right date. Everyone assumed that he'd found the perfect woman for him. At least for now.

"Your father seems happy," he said to her as they walked away from the buffet table.

"That might have something to do with Mrs. Claus," Amy said, looking at Joyce. She'd obviously sprayed something on her strawberry blond hair to make it gray for tonight. The red-and-green dress and white apron, coupled with a jaunty white ruffled cap, made her look just like Santa's most important helper.

"They make a cute couple."

"Funny," Amy said, giving him a crooked grin, "they say the same thing about us."

They're right, Gray wanted to say, but knew this wasn't the time. Amy was trying much harder than he was to keep their relationship impersonal. Either that, or she simply wasn't as interested in him as he was in her. Given her response whenever they were alone and when he'd kissed her, he didn't think so. He hoped she'd see the advantages of changing their relationship from pretend dating to something more mutually satisfying.

"I'd love a cola rather than any more of that sweet punch," Amy said. "Let's see if the machine is working."

They headed for the dimly lit hallway in back of the kitchen. "You're probably tired," Gray said. "You've been on your feet on that hard floor for over an hour."

"I'm used to it. Doctors often have to stand for surgery or exams. But you've put in a full day, too."

He produced a handful of coins and Amy selected two soft drinks from the machine.

"Let's grab a seat on the steps," she said.

Tucking her skirt around her legs, she settled on the step and brushed off the space beside her. "When

I was a little girl, I used to hide out here during some of the sermons.''

''Not all of them? I played hooky from church on a regular basis.''

''No,'' she said, her eyes focusing on something he couldn't see, something far in her past. ''My father sang in the choir, so I usually sat with friends and their families. When the minister talked about death, I didn't want to hear the words. I know they were meant to be comforting, but I missed my mother too much to hear such abstract thoughts. All I could think about was how alone I felt.''

''You never had brothers or sisters, right?''

''Right. I think my mother would have liked more children, but I was all they had.''

''I was an only child, too. I know how that feels.''

''Did you have imaginary friends?'' Amy asked, turning her head toward him.

''Of course. Sometimes I had an entire fantasy baseball team. We went to the Little League championships more than once.''

Amy chuckled. ''I had a big brother who went on grand adventures with me. Sometimes he made me feel less alone at night, when my dad had to go out for an emergency.''

''He left you alone?''

''I was at least twelve then,'' she explained, ''when most girls are baby-sitting for other children. Besides, this is a small town, where crime was practically nonexistent. I wasn't too young to stay at home, but I was kind of a baby about being alone at night.''

''I don't think you were a baby.''

"Thanks, but looking back, I really was. I wasn't worried about somebody breaking in to the house, or something bad happening to me. I was worried about my father, and how I'd feel if I lost him too."

Gray placed an arm around Amy's shoulders. "I think I understand. I didn't have the same experience, of course, since both my parents were alive, but my mother seemed to worry excessively."

"About herself?"

"No, about me. Unlike your mother, I don't think she wanted any more children. She put all her eggs in one basket, so to speak, and she definitely guarded that basket."

"I suppose overprotective is better than complacent."

"That's a very adult way to look at it. As a child, I wasn't nearly that objective."

Amy chuckled again. "I understand. Sometimes it's difficult for a parent to let their child have the freedom to either succeed or fail on their own."

"Exactly."

"Which is probably why you established your own company as an adult."

"I hadn't thought about it, but you may be right."

"We only children have our own experiences, don't we?"

He looked into her eyes, which appeared a dark indigo in the low light of the hallway. They had more in common than he'd once thought. He felt a closeness to Amy he hadn't felt in ages, if ever. Without thinking, he tightened his arm around her shoulders.

To hell with good intentions, he thought as his gaze shifted from her eyes to her full, beautifully sculpted mouth. He remembered how the upper bow of her lips, so smooth and distinct, felt when his mouth had settled over hers. He longed to trace the shape again with his tongue, to taste the sweetness of the soda she'd sipped and savor her unique flavor. He angled closer, against the steps, his gaze caressing the soft pink blush of her cheeks. When he looked into her eyes, he discovered her startled awareness and more than a hint of matching passion.

Oh, yes, she wanted him too. Inside the darkened interior of his car or on the dimly lit steps of the church back hallway. His heart pounded hard and fast and he felt himself swell with desire.

"I'd better get back to the cookies," she said suddenly, breathlessly, jumping up from the step. "I'll bet Thelma is ready for a break."

"I'll be there in a minute," he said with a sigh as she practically ran toward the large gathering of friends and neighbors.

Gray sucked in a series of deep breaths, willing himself to calm down. When he decided he wouldn't embarrass himself or Amy, he pushed himself up to follow her down the hall. Probably just as well that she'd run from what was certain to be a very hot kiss—and perhaps an even hotter night ahead. He'd kept his hands to himself for weeks, but he was only human. Amy was more temptation than he'd ever had to resist.

"THE PARTY WAS A LOT OF fun," Gray said as he pulled his Lexus to a stop in Amy's driveway. "Thanks for inviting me."

The earlier tension they'd felt when they'd sat on

the back steps had disappeared, replaced with the polite social behavior she associated with Gray. She was glad, she told herself. She didn't want a lover, even one as tempting and charming as Gray.

"I'm glad you went with me," she said, equally determined to be warm and civil. "My father seemed to have a special gleam in his eyes when he saw you there."

"He makes a good Santa."

"Since he's gained a little weight around his middle, he doesn't need as much padding any more," Amy said, remembering the times she'd helped him dress in the red suit after she'd discovered *he,* not some Santa surrogate from the North Pole, was playing the jolly old elf.

She unbuckled her seat belt and turned toward Gray. "Would you like to come in for coffee?"

Gray stilled, as though she'd asked him an especially difficult question. Well, maybe she had. They hadn't been truly alone, except in the car, for a long time.

"Just coffee and some conversation," she added when he continued to study her in the dim light of the car's interior. "I'd really like to discuss something with you."

"All right," he said, slipping the key from the ignition.

She didn't wait for him to come around to her side of the car, as he usually did when they were out in public. Although she appreciated the polite gesture, it made her feel too special. Too much like a real, cherished date.

She felt his strong, warm presence at her back

while she unlocked the front door. Her fingers seemed especially clumsy as she jiggled the lock, then finally heard the dead bolt slide free.

Slipping inside quickly, she found the switch and flooded the small entryway with light. "Make yourself comfortable," she said over her shoulder as she shrugged out of her coat. "I'll just be a minute."

His hands caught the collar, easing it off her arms. She was reminded of their first date not too long ago, when he'd helped her on with her coat. She'd been nervous for another reason that night, but just as strongly aware of his overwhelming presence.

"Thanks," she said breathlessly. "I'll have the coffee ready in a moment."

"No hurry," he said as she fled to the kitchen.

A few minutes later, she entered the living room with two mugs. "Cream, no sugar, right?"

"That's right," he said, taking the warm mug and enclosing her fingers in his personal heat for just a moment. Her heart raced, darn it, just when she'd managed to get herself under control when she was alone in the kitchen. Was there no way to be around Gray without wanting him?

"I was just looking over your CDs," Gray said, taking his coffee to the sofa and sitting down. "You've done a lot more unpacking than when I was here a few weeks ago."

"I've managed to work some in," she said, sitting at the other end of the couch, "but I have to admit it's not my favorite leisure activity."

Gray looked at her with hooded silver eyes over the rim of his mug. "I won't make any comments about what you might rather be doing."

Amy sucked in a deep breath. Ridiculous. She interpreted everything the man said as a suggestive comment. Surely he wasn't always implying something sexual!

"Regarding activities outside my practice," she said, pulling professionalism around her like a shield against his charisma, "I wanted to talk about our dates."

"I think they've been going well."

"For the most part, I'd agree."

He sat up straighter. "What do you mean?"

"I mean that we agreed to *pretend* to be dating. We weren't supposed to actually be in a relationship."

"So you object to us enjoying each other's company?" He sounded very defensive. Perhaps she wasn't handling this well.

"Of course not. I'm thrilled that we have a good time when we're together. What worries me is the type and number of our dates. I just believe that perhaps we're losing focus on why we're spending time together."

"Maybe having a good time is enough."

She shook her head. "That's not what we agreed."

"I don't remember agreeing to have a specific number of dates, and then not having a good time on those," he replied, leaning forward and placing his mug on the coffee table.

"Gray, that's not what I meant," she said with a sigh. "I'm just worried that we're turning this pretend dating into the actual thing."

"You mean you think I'm the one who's lost focus of our goal."

"Well...no. I'm just as guilty. I certainly haven't discouraged a more...friendly relationship. Maybe I've simply recognized the problem first."

"You see our dates as a problem?"

"I didn't say that!"

He rose from the couch and paced the length of her small living room. The journey took only a few strides, then he was back, standing before her chair. "Amy, I'm not going to apologize for liking you as a person. Or for wanting to spend time with you."

"I'm not asking you to. I've enjoyed our dates. I've enjoyed...you."

Gray looked at her long and hard, his gaze glittering with unnamed emotion. Or maybe just desire. How could she tell when she knew so little about what he was feeling? But did she *want* to know? She'd just explained how they shouldn't really be dating. If she followed her own advice, she'd keep her distance. She wouldn't complicate their relationship by delving into his reasons and innermost feelings.

"Tell me again why we should stick to the agreement? Why we shouldn't explore this attraction we both feel?" Gray finally said, his voice as soft and rich as melting butter.

Amy took a deep breath. "Because we have goals. Because you don't want a long-term relationship, and I don't want an affair."

Gray reached down and pulled her to her feet. Her breasts brushed his chest, and her skirt swirled against his hard thighs. She remembered how good he'd felt when they'd danced, how wonderful he kissed. Would it be so wrong to give in to the feelings, just for a moment?

Her breasts ached from the friction of their breathing. Heavy, hot breathing. Gray's eyes glittered with barely restrained desire as she stared up into his handsome, hard-planed face. She wanted him. He wanted her. Could she resist such compelling passion?

Yes! She had to be strong. Strong enough for both of them.

Amazingly, her legs supported her. She wondered if her feet would obey her if she ordered them to run away.

"Are you so sure, Amy?"

"About what?" Her voice sounded faint, breathless.

"About not wanting an affair. We're two consenting adults with a right to a private life. Who would we be hurting?"

She closed her eyes, breathing in the clean, crisp scent of him, feeling his warmth so close, so strong. The touch of his finger on her chin snapped her eyes open.

"Amy?"

Did he know how much she desired him, how much she wanted to give in to the physical demands of her body? "We'd be hurting ourselves, Gray. I can't have that kind of relationship with you and not crave more. And knowing that there was no future for us would break my heart."

"Why?" He sounded genuinely curious, as though the concept was as foreign to him as the reality of having a casual affair was to her.

"Because I care too much about you as it is. I'm not willing to set myself up for heartache."

He stroked her jaw with his fingers, briefly resting his palm against her cheek. Then he stepped back, taking his warmth and strength with him. "I can't promise you more than good times and great sex."

Chapter Seven

"I'm not asking for anything, Gray, except your acceptance of our agreement. Or if you want to get out, just say so. I'll tell my father we had an argument, or a disagreement. Or you can come up with a story." She shook her head. "Please don't make me sound too mean or unreasonable."

"I'm not about to tell stories about you."

"Then what do you want to do?"

He ran a hand through his hair. "I think we should continue with our agreement. I'll do my best to stick to the terms if you'll promise to remind me if I stray."

"And you do the same for me," she answered with a sigh, turning away. She'd gotten what she wanted, hadn't she? So why did she feel so depressed? Why did she want to fling her arms around Gray, ask him to stay—the agreement be damned?

She couldn't allow herself to act impulsively. Since the age of eleven, she'd been responsible. First for simple meals, then for coordinating social events. She'd been the "woman" of the household, taking care of her dad as her mother had done before her death: scolding, praising and cajoling as needed to make things run smoothly.

He'd been busy with his practice and distracted over his grief, but he'd been a good father. They'd settled into a quiet, comfortable life, but deep down inside, she'd worried that something might happen to him. A car wreck, like the one that killed her mother, when he was going to or returning from a house call. Or a sudden illness; he was, after all, getting older.

Amy smiled to herself. When she was barely a teenager, a person nearing fifty seemed old indeed.

"What's so funny?" Gray asked from across the small room. His hands in his pants pockets, he seemed far different from the overwhelming man who had pulled her close just minutes before. She marveled again at how quickly and easily Gray could change personas.

"Oh, I was just remembering my father. How we'd been through a lot together when my mother died."

"He's proud of you. I saw it in his eyes tonight."

"He's happy with you, too." Amy collected the two mugs, intent on staying busy and away from any more tempting situations. "He thinks you're a great catch."

"Almost good enough for his little girl."

Amy grinned, relieved that Gray no longer seemed angry or frustrated. "Almost."

"Then I guess we'd better keep him happy."

"Yes, we'd better." She sighed. "The best thing would probably be to avoid all...personal situations.

Just the regularly scheduled dates that the town will see.''

Gray took a deep breath. ''If that's what you think is best.''

''I really don't see any alternative.''

He stepped a little closer, raising his hand to her cheek. His warm palm cradled her jaw as his eyes softened from silver to aged pewter. ''Let me know if you change your mind.''

AMBROSE STEERED HIS CAR to a stop in Joyce's driveway. The glow of her multicolored Christmas lights around the eaves and window of the beauty shop illuminated the inside of the car after he turned off the engine. Her house was behind the frame business, shielded by a live oak tree and a path lined with shrubs.

Not that he'd been asked inside...yet.

''I had a lovely time tonight, Ambrose,'' she said, breaking into his contemplation of her neat, tidy world. Would she welcome change at this stage in her life, or was she settled into her house? A year ago he wouldn't have considered changing much about how he lived, but since he'd broken his ankle and Amy had moved back to town, he'd been thinking about the rut he'd gotten himself into.

''Joyce, you don't think I'm too old to be makin' some changes, do you?''

''Why, that depends, I suppose. What kind of changes?''

He looked at the charming lady beside him. ''I'm not about to get my nose pierced or buy a motorcycle, if that's what you're askin'. I just don't want to be some old coot with the same ratty furniture and shiny-knee pants he's had for the past twenty years.''

''Oh, Ambrose, that's not you! Why, you're a respected member of this community, a talented medical doctor. No one thinks you're an old coot!''

''I'm not too worried about what everyone else thinks, Joyce,'' he said, gripping the steering wheel so he didn't grab her hand. ''I'm kind of concerned about your opinion.''

''Why, I...Ambrose, are you asking me about my feelings for you?''

He squirmed in the bench seat as a wave of heat rushed up his neck to his face. Darn it, but with those confounded Christmas lights, she'd be able to see how flustered he was. ''Not exactly,'' he hedged, ''but I'd be sorely disappointed if you thought I was spendin' time with you for the wrong reasons.''

''And what would those reasons be?''

He shrugged. ''Like I didn't have anythin' better to do. I do, you know.''

She frowned, her eyes revealing his mistake.

''I didn't mean that! I don't have one darn thing to do that I'd rather be doin' than spend time with you.''

''Ambrose, you are one exasperating man.''

He shook his head. ''I know I am, Joyce. Just try to have some patience with me, okay? I haven't wooed a woman in forty years.''

''I'm glad I finally know what you're doing,'' she said, amusement warring with annoyance.

''Well, I'm not so sure I know what I'm doin', so just have patience with me a little longer, okay? I'm tryin' to get the hang of this datin' thing.''

She chuckled in that deep, throaty way she had of making him feel decades younger than his sixty some years. "I just hope you get the hang of it better than your daughter's young man. He doesn't seem to know how to get from first base to third, if you know what I mean."

"Joyce, that's my baby girl you're talkin' about!"

"Sorry, Ambrose, but I have to speak my mind. Thelma and I had high hopes of a promising romance by Christmas, but nothing is happening."

"They've been out on at least two dates a week for the past month."

"But where are they going? To Bretford House or Wimberly, for dinner. Why, he has her home by ten o'clock every night. You'd think she was back in the tenth grade."

"I respect that in him. He's not rushin' my daughter into some meanin'less affair."

"Ambrose, he's not making *any* moves! They haven't been alone together since the Christmas party at the church, and I'm not sure that counts because they were in the community center the whole time. Why, they spent more time together on their first date than they have in the past few weeks."

"He's a gentleman."

Joyce took a deep breath. "I thought you wanted a son-in-law and some grandbabies?"

Ambrose thought about it for a moment. He wanted Amy to find a special man, someone who would love and appreciate her. On the other hand, he didn't want her to wait until she was too old to experience the joy of having children. Amy was a warm and generous woman who would make a wonderful mother. The sooner, the better.

Joyce was right; he had to keep his priorities straight. ''Maybe you have a point.''

''I know we do. Thelma and I have talked about it, and we've decided Amy and Gray need a little boost.''

Ambrose leaned forward in the seat and smiled, his own budding romance pushed aside for the moment. ''What did you two matchmakers come up with?''

IN THE REMAINING DAYS before Christmas, Amy barely had time to keep up with the increased cases of colds, flu and upper respiratory infections. Her father was able to see more patients as his ankle improved, but a combination of the weather and the holiday season conspired to bring more people into the clinic than was normal. Amy even had to cancel her Wednesday afternoon off to keep up with the workload.

The town seemed to be celebrating the holiday season excessively, inviting her and Gray to everything from small dinners to Chamber of Commerce parties. He'd been a real sport, arranging his work schedule so he was available for early evening events. He'd delegated some responsibilities to his managers so he didn't need to leave town. From his comments regarding his company, Amy believed the move to Ranger Springs had benefitted both his business and his personal life.

Tonight he'd escort her to a small party at the Four Square Café hosted by Thelma for *Springs Gazette* employees and special guests. The opportunity to get photos into the paper was not to be missed, the editor had added when she'd cornered Amy and Gray at the Chamber of Commerce Christmas party. Gray had graciously accepted the invitation, no doubt thinking of the free publicity any photo would bring his company.

Their dates had become social events. He hadn't made any personal suggestions for Christmas shopping trips or quiet dinners away from the public eye. He hadn't given her intimate looks, held her hand when they were alone, or otherwise made her feel as though they were actually a couple. She was grateful, and yet...

With another sigh, she plopped down on her sofa. She missed the quiet anticipation of spending time with him away from the prying eyes of her friends and neighbors. Her body yearned for the sexually charged moments they'd shared on the dance floor and in his car on their first date. She longed for the excitement of finding him in the clinic's waiting room, or having lunch at the café.

"I miss him," she whispered to herself. They'd been in the same room, at the same party, but they hadn't been alone. Not that he'd ignored her. He'd been polite and charming, as though she were his first cousin.

Maybe she shouldn't have been so emphatic about not pursuing a relationship outside the bounds of their agreement. If she'd been a little more open to seeing him privately, or spending time alone just because they enjoyed each other's company, perhaps they could have explored where their dating might lead. Maybe he wasn't really opposed to finding someone special for his life.

No, she reminded herself, shaking her head, he'd been very clear. She would be deluding herself if she thought there was a future together for her and Gray. Despite having a few things in common, such as growing up only children and being determined to make a life here in Ranger Springs, they were very different. Gray's dedication to his business might appear similar to her dedication to medicine, but he took his role as founder and president of Grayson Industries as seriously as most men took their marriages.

He'd claimed he made a terrible husband. If he ignored his wife for his business, Amy could well imagine that he was correct.

Or maybe he'd been married to the wrong woman. Maybe… No, her speculation was ridiculous. Women didn't change workaholics into perfectly attentive husbands; men had to make that decision on their own.

The sound of his car in her driveway broke into her thoughts. She pushed up from the couch, wondering for the hundredth time why she'd purchased something so uncomfortable. Black leather had seemed cosmopolitan and appropriate for a single woman in Fort Worth. In her cozy little frame house in Ranger Springs, it seemed ridiculous.

Before Gray rang her doorbell, she smoothed her black silk shirt over matching slim pants. A cheerful, colorful Christmas tree pin kept the outfit from appearing too severe. With all the social events she and

Gray had attended in the past weeks, she was running out of clothing changes!

"Hello," she said as she eased open the door. A cold north wind ruffled his salt-and-pepper hair and gave color to his lean cheeks as he climbed the steps. The same wind plastered the thin silk to her shivering body.

"Hello." He paused, giving her a quick once-over that instantly took away the winter's chill. "You look wonderful."

"Thank you. Please, come inside." She backed up, but couldn't escape a slight brush against his warm, hard body as he held the door open. Longing for the electrifying attraction she'd experienced only with Gray hit her hard. All she had to do was lean forward, press her breasts against his chest, slide her hands beneath the soft wool of his jacket.... All she had to say was that she'd decided to void their agreement. They could have a meaningless but mutually satisfying affair. They could be discreet. No one needed to know they were warming each others' sheets but the two of them....

And yet she knew such bravado would be a lie. Sex with Gray would be anything but simple, and she was sure everyone in town would know of her joy and her ultimate heartache.

She couldn't risk her heart any more than her reputation. For years, she'd guarded both zealously.

He held out her coat. "Are you ready?"

Ready for another party. Another social obligation where they could act the part of the happy couple for the whole town to see. Ready? No, she wasn't, she wanted to say. Let's just stay home and cuddle on the couch. Let's heat up that cool black leather and forget the agreement. Instead, Amy made herself smile in reply as she slid her arm into the sleeve. "Of course."

AMY'S TENSION INCREASED as December waned. Her schedule remained busy at the clinic, but at least the holiday social invitations decreased as families prepared for Christmas celebrations and trips. She thought she saw conjecture about herself and Gray in the eyes of her friends and neighbors, but perhaps that was her imagination. Was the tension coming from her desire to be with him—and knowing she had to keep her hands off—or from the pressure of others wanting them to become even closer?

An uncomfortable and potentially disastrous Christmas family celebration was avoided when Gray announced he'd be going back to Dallas for the holiday. He would spend the long weekend with his mother and stepfather.

Amy breathed a sigh of relief that she wouldn't have to endure more speculative looks from her father and Joyce, who'd agreed to join them for dinner at the Wheatley home. When presents were opened, no one would be looking over her shoulder to see if Gray had purchased some pricey piece of jewelry. She wouldn't have to explain that her gift to Gray was neither expensive nor extremely personal; she'd had a difficult time finding something for a man who was her pretend boyfriend. However, she was rather proud of her selection, although there had been a lot of rushing to get it finished on time.

Before he'd left, he'd asked if they could exchange

gifts when he returned on Tuesday. He probably didn't know what to get for her, either. No doubt he'd buy a gift similar to what he would give a secretary or a female friend. A scarf or a pair of leather gloves, maybe.

The smell of roasted turkey and dressing drifted through the open doorway of the kitchen. From the adjoining living room, Christmas carols provided background music for her father's conversations with Joyce. Amy placed the last of the embroidered Christmas napkins beside each place setting, then straightened a knife that had been bumped out of place. Ready.

Just like she'd done for many years as a teenager, she'd set the table and prepared a meal for herself and her father. She'd placed the centerpiece of red silk poinsettias and striped candy canes on a table runner embossed with peppermint sticks and snowmen. Childhood comforts, kept from when her mother had performed the routine each Christmas.

In the past, the sameness had seemed comforting for both her and her father. This year, however, they had company. For the first time Ambrose Wheatley had invited a woman to share the holiday with them. A signal, perhaps, that he was ready to move on? That his daughter should do the same?

Amy wasn't sure. Something felt different about this holiday, but she couldn't tell if it was her move back to Ranger Springs after years away, or her father's love interest or her own mixed feelings about Gray. The people, the music, and the decorations were the same, but she was seeing them through the eyes of a nearly thirty-year-old woman, not a twelve-year-old girl. This year, she wished she'd splurged on a new table decoration or changed the menu just a little. Did her newfound restlessness extend beyond the Christmas holiday? Did she want more from her personal life as well?

GRAY NEEDED THE THREE days away from Ranger Springs to get perspective on this situation he'd gotten himself into with Amy. Who would have believed he'd be so attracted to a dedicated small-town doctor? At the time they'd made their agreement, he hadn't expected to become emotionally attached to her. He'd liked her from their first date, but since the divorce he'd been able to keep women in perspective; his business and all that entailed came first.

He'd encouraged Amy to think about an affair. Had he been thinking with that supposedly sharp mind of his, or with another part of his anatomy? After being away from her for two days, away from the pressures of Ranger Springs matchmakers, did he still believe an affair was possible?

The present he'd purchased for her yesterday rested on the dresser of his old bedroom at the family home in east Dallas—the one his mother had kept in the divorce. Wrapped in elegant black and gold, he wondered if Amy would like his gift selection. He wondered if she'd think it was too much, too soon. He'd find out on Tuesday.

"Gray, dinner is almost ready," his mother said from the open doorway. "Your stepfather and our guests are finishing their cocktails."

He turned, chasing away his worries with a pleasant smile. He didn't want to hint at anything that would upset her on Christmas. "I'll be right there, Mother."

"I'm so glad you came home for the holiday."

"I am too," he said with a genuine smile. His mother smiled in return, showing her perfect dimples unaffected by a recent facelift. She smoothed the lapels on her tailored silk suit and turned back to her guests.

Gray sighed. He couldn't tell her that his need to be back in Dallas—and out of Ranger Springs—was twofold. First, he sincerely believed one should be with family during the holidays. Since his father was in the Mediterranean with his very young third wife, visiting him wasn't an option. Second, he needed the time away from Amy. Away from the tension of wanting her, of knowing their dating agreement kept them apart even as it pulled them together, time after time.

Suddenly, he needed to talk to her. To wish her a Merry Christmas and hear her voice. The holiday dinner could wait just two or three minutes while he made a call to Ranger Springs.

He dialed information to get Ambrose Wheatley's home number, then counted the rings impatiently until someone answered. He knew Amy was at her family home; she'd mentioned that Joyce was joining her and her father for the meal.

"Hello?" Her voice sounded warm and slightly breathless. Sexy as hell.

"It's Gray," he said, clenching the phone tightly.

"Is everything okay?"

"Fine. I just wanted to talk to you. To wish you a Merry Christmas."

He imagined her face softening from an expression of worry to the slight smile she wore as naturally as a white lab coat. "Merry Christmas to you, too," she said, her voice as soothing and inviting as her smile.

"I'm looking forward to seeing you tomorrow. I know it's against our agreement, but this is, after all, a special holiday."

"I...I understand. There's no need to exchange gifts at the town square."

"I'm glad you understand." He paused, elated that the conversation was going so well. Good enough that he could press for more. "How about dinner? You've never been out to my house, and I'd like to show you how the art looks in the dining room."

She paused as though considering the implications of being alone in his house. "You're cooking?" she finally said.

"Yes."

"That's worth one minor violation of our agreement. I remember those omelettes you fixed in the cabin."

"I'll try to live up to your expectations." *In more ways than one,* he felt like adding.

"All right," she said, her voice both hesitant and husky.

She could turn him on with little more than a simple comment, an innocent remark. "I'll see you around five o'clock, then, at my house. You are off tomorrow, aren't you?"

"Yes, the clinic is closed. I'll put my dad on call."

"See you tomorrow," he said in a near whisper, wishing she were here right now, in his old bedroom, with her competent hands and soft smiles. Wishing he could stretch out beside her on that queen-size bed and explore all the places he'd dreamed about with increasing frequency.

He heard a faint sigh on the line. "Merry Christmas, Gray."

"Merry Christmas. See you tomorrow." He placed the receiver back on the phone cradle.

He'd agreed to their relationship to escape the demands of unending blind dates. He'd thought his life was complicated back then. He'd believed those dates were creating a problem in his personal life.

He'd been clueless. He now realized the biggest problem he'd encountered since the divorce was wanting a woman he couldn't have for several valid reasons—and having a very strong desire to toss all his good intentions and logical arguments out the window.

But he didn't want to get married again. The idea of a wife and family still sent chills through him. He knew he'd be a terrible husband. Hadn't he proved so in the past? Since he'd had such bad role models, he'd no doubt be an equally terrible father. He couldn't risk another bad marriage just because he wanted Amy Wheatley more than he'd wanted anything in a long, long time.

Chapter Eight

As soon as Amy turned off the key to her car, she placed a hand across her stomach, as though she could quiet the fluttering inside. Okay, she'd been over this before, deciding she could handle a violation of their agreement. Or maybe a total change in their agreement. They were exchanging gifts in private. He was cooking dinner for her.

Apparently, with a little help from Hanson's Air Conditioning and Heating. Glancing at the repair truck parked outside Gray's home, she hoped he didn't have a serious problem.

The weak winter sun rested wearily on the endless hills to the west. Until Christmas Eve, the weather had been warm, but now a cold front had pushed south until everyone wondered if they might get a rare snowfall. No such luck, Amy thought as she grabbed the large gift bag, pulled her jacket tight and hurried toward the front door.

The door opened when she was halfway up the fieldstone steps. One of her former schoolmates, Tug Hanson, nearly hit her in the shins with his metal tool case.

"Oops," he said, a big smile on his homely face. "I nearly got you, Amy." He sat the heavy box down with a rattle.

"You sure did, Tug." She peered past him to the open doorway. "Gray?"

"Right here," he said, easing through the opening. "We had a little problem."

"Anything serious?"

"I don't think so," Gray replied.

"Wind blew out the pilot light on the furnace sometime this weekend," Tug explained. "I put on a gizmo that'll keep it from happening again and relit the pilot." He grinned, giving a trademark pull on his left ear.

A gizmo, hmm? She certainly hoped Tug knew his heating repairs better than he knew the proper names of the mechanical components he installed.

"We're all finished, then?" Gray asked.

"You bet." Tug picked up his tool case and gave her a wave. "Good to see you again, Amy."

"Same here, Tug."

Gray stood outside the door, an intense, welcoming smile on his face. He looked wonderful, dressed in a black pullover sweater and faded jeans that hugged his hips and thighs. Lean and hard and just a tiny bit edgy. "Come inside."

Said the spider to the fly, Amy thought as she walked up the remaining steps. The sound of the van leaving faded into the distance as she stood in front of Gray.

"Are you sure this is a good time for you? I could come back some other—"

"Today is fine. The temperature inside is a little

cool,'' he said as he pushed the door wider, ''but I've built a fire.''

As soon as she walked into the house, the smell of some type of aromatic sauce hit her hard. Maybe those fluttering sensations in her stomach were really hunger pangs.

''You might want to leave your jacket on for a while,'' Gray said as he placed a hand on her back. ''The furnace will warm the place up in a half hour or so, according to our resident expert.''

''It's not so cold,'' Amy said, walking across the stone-paved foyer so she could see the open floor plan. To her left, the large living room stretched upwards toward a loft, accessed by a curving staircase. A wall of windows overlooked the Hill Country. To the right, a dining room provided a more intimate space, with seating for eight around a highly polished, dark wood table. Two places had been set at the end, near another window that overlooked the rolling hills.

''Your home is beautiful.'' She loved the blend of natural elements and open space.

''Thank you. I've enjoyed it.'' He walked into the dining room. ''What do you think?''

She followed him, her gaze fixing on the large framed mixed media piece that hung over an antique sideboard. ''It's perfect. You have a good eye.''

''Robin helped me understand what I like. She's really good at working with people.''

''I'm sure she is.'' Amy knew it would be a while before she could afford an interior decorator. She still had some student loans to pay off, then she'd like to invest more in equipment for the clinic. First to go when she did have extra money would be the leather couch. "She's a friend, also, isn't she?"

Gray nodded. "I was best man in her wedding to Ethan."

"Have you known him a long time?" Amy asked as she followed him through a short hall into the kitchen.

"We met in Dallas, while I was working on a project for the FBI." Gray walked over to a professional looking stove and picked up a wooden spoon. "At the time, I was married and he was single, so we didn't socialize as much as we would have if we'd both been unattached."

"So now that you've moved to Ranger Springs, he's married and you're single."

"Life's funny that way," Gray said, stirring the fragrant sauce. He left the spoon in the pot and opened another lid. Steam wafted toward a copper vent.

"My goodness, that smells good."

"A family recipe."

"Is your mother a good cook?"

"No, but our housekeeper was," Gray replied with a smile. "She was determined I'd be able to prepare a few dishes so I wouldn't live on pizza and burgers when I got my first apartment." He shrugged. "I realized I enjoyed puttering around the kitchen, especially after the divorce."

He spoke of the breakup of his marriage without any emotion, but Amy wondered if deep inside he still had scars. He'd seemed bitter when he spoke of his ex-wife, but not when he spoke of being married. That probably said something profound about him, but she didn't know if she wanted to pursue that line of thinking. Somehow, delving into his past seemed too intrusive. She was more interested in his present, anyway.

"Let me open some wine, then I'll get the salads."

"I'll help."

He pointed toward the refrigerator. "Second shelf. The dressing is in the small carafe."

Within a few minutes, they had everything in place on the dining room table. Gray walked to one of the chairs and pulled it out for her.

"I could get very spoiled," she teased as she eased into the comfortable upholstered seat.

"That's my goal," he said easily. Again, Amy wondered how much she could read into his glib remarks. Was he saying those phrases because he really was the best date anyone had every imagined, or did he believe he should treat every woman as special? Or maybe he had another reason… something she hadn't imagined yet.

They sipped a rich red wine and ate salad, then pasta. Amy didn't know what he'd put in the delicious sauce, but she was pretty sure the ingredients weren't on her utilitarian kitchen shelves. Her cooking skills were adequate for herself and her father—when she'd still lived at home—but hardly qualified as gourmet. Gray hadn't learned to prepare that pasta dish as a bachelor recipe from the family housekeeper. He apparently took cooking as seriously as he took everything else, intent on being the best.

"How was your visit in Dallas?" she asked to break the silence.

"Cordial. How was your Christmas dinner?"

"Fun. I fixed the usual—turkey, stuffing, green beans, mashed potatoes—and Daddy ate too much, also as usual. Joyce seemed to have a good time. I think she and my father are pretty serious."

"Good for them. Are you okay with their relationship?"

"I believe so. I'm glad that my father is getting involved with someone again, and I can't think of a nicer lady than Joyce." She paused, twirling a bite of pasta in the last of the sauce. "How about your parents?"

"My stepfather cursed online trading and the Democrats. My mother looks fabulous after her face-lift. The family home is exactly the same, with the exception of the new satellite dish in back of the pool." He took a sip of wine. "I had a nice visit."

"What about your father?"

"Cruising the Mediterranean with wife number three. He sent a card from Crete."

"I'm sorry you're not closer."

Gray shrugged. "We all try, in our own way, I suppose. I can't help wondering what life would have been like if they'd stayed married. If they hadn't used me as some kind of trophy they both wanted, but then had little use for."

"Parents are sometimes so caught up in their own pain they don't consider the effect on the children."

"I know, and as an adult, I see that clearly. I realize, however, that a part of me is always going to be a ten-year-old child where my parents are concerned."

"At least you have a relationship with both of

them. Maybe not a Norman Rockwell ideal family unit, but you're speaking."

"And that's an astute commentary on modern life."

"Not everyone gets divorced."

Gray shrugged. "It seems to run in my family, like premature gray hair."

Amy didn't believe that for a minute, but she wasn't about to argue the point. Gray had strong views on marriage and family, and nothing she said would change his mind.

"That was a wonderful post-Christmas meal," she said as she placed her napkin beside the plate. "I wasn't up for turkey and dressing sandwiches quite yet."

"Sounds…interesting," Gray said with a chuckle, pushing back from the table. "I'll have to try that some day."

She almost said she'd fix him one, but then she'd be inviting him to dinner, and who knew what would develop from that point. No, better to keep the relationship simple. After all, they weren't really dating, even if they were involved.

Attracted, she corrected as he pulled out her chair. His subtle cologne, so fresh and woodsy, combined with his heat to send her heart racing. She concentrated on not stumbling as she stood up. To keep her hands busy and off his firm chest and shoulders, she grabbed her dinner and salad plates.

"You don't need to—"

"No, I want to help," she said in a rush. "After all, you did all the cooking."

When she looked into his eyes, she knew she

hadn't fooled him for a minute. He knew she was uncomfortable around him, at least when they were alone. He knew she fought the attraction constantly.

Maybe she was tired of fighting.

CLEANING UP THE KITCHEN took little time. Before Amy could check out all the modern appliances and fully appreciate the hand-painted tile, Gray had escorted her into the living room with a cup of hazelnut coffee. He added a few logs to the dwindling fire, despite the fact the furnace now seemed to be working.

"You didn't put up a tree," Amy observed as they settled onto Gray's couch. His comfortable, cushy upholstered couch, she silently added. She simply had to get one of these soon.

"Since I'm not home all that much, I didn't see the need. Besides," he added with a smile, "I've seen more than my share of decorated Christmas trees in these past few weeks."

Amy smiled as she took a sip of her coffee. "We have seen a few."

"Every one in Ranger Springs," Gray added.

"You haven't seen my father's," she said impulsively, then wished she could take back the words. She was practically suggesting they violate their agreement again. "I mean, it's decorated with all my school projects from elementary school, plus a collection of cartoon ornaments I started collecting when I was about ten. Believe me, that tree is always a sight."

"I'll bet it's cute," Gray said, his eyes dancing

with mischief. ‘‘I’ll bet you were cute when you were a little girl.’’

‘‘I was gangly and had braces,’’ she informed him.

‘‘So now you’re leggy and have a beautiful smile.’’

Amy felt herself blush—not a common occurrence in her life. ‘‘Thank you, but I think I’m pretty average.’’

‘‘Still comparing yourself to Maryanne, hmm?’’ He took the cup from her hand and set it on the table. Before she could think of an intelligent comment, he took her hands in his. ‘‘You know what I told you before,’’ he gently chided. ‘‘You’re a natural beauty. She does what she can to make herself as attractive as you are without obsessing over your looks.’’

‘‘Gray, I…’’

‘‘You’re going to tell me I’m violating the agreement again, aren’t you?’’

‘‘The thought crossed my mind,’’ she whispered.

‘‘I’m beginning to regret that agreement.’’

‘‘I have a confession,’’ she said softly. ‘‘Sometimes…sometimes I feel the same way.’’

‘‘What are you saying?’’

‘‘That I wonder what might have happened if we hadn’t been pretending for the past month or so. If you didn’t have the one-date rule. What if we could have explored our attraction and seen where it led?’’

‘‘I can tell you right now where it would lead,’’ Gray said, pulling her closer and placing her hands on his shoulders. ‘‘Up the steps to that loft.’’

‘‘Are you that sure?’’

‘‘Yes.’’

His hand stroked her back, feeling heavenly

against the silk of her blouse. "Even though you'd vowed not to get involved with anyone."

"Sometimes men say foolish things."

"You mean when they're thinking with their heads and not some other part of their bodies?"

He slowly urged her closer. "Right."

"I always thought it was the other way around."

"No, I think I should have followed my original instincts and seduced you immediately. I've always wanted to take a beautiful woman to that cabin and have my wicked way with her."

Amy smiled, feeling feminine power like she'd never experienced before. "You think I would have been receptive to those caveman tactics?"

"I would have been very civilized, but very insistent."

"And now? What kind of strategy would you use?"

He seemed surprised for a moment, his hands stilling. "I'm considerably more frustrated right now than I was a month ago. I might rush things."

"Really?" she asked, curling her fingers into his chest.

"I'd try very hard not to be a caveman."

Her sensitive breasts touched his chest. "What if I wanted to see that side of you?"

"You don't like the side of me you've seen so far?"

"Oh, I like it very much. But I know there's something else, something hidden deep inside that you rarely let anyone see."

"I think maybe you're imagining this other side of me."

"I think not."

"Amy, don't try to conceive of me as someone I'm not. I haven't lied to you about anything—my background, my plans, my feelings on commitment."

"I know you haven't lied. I admire that about you, Gray. But I also believe there's more to you than what you show to the world. Or even to me."

"I can't be who you want me to be. Who you need."

"Maybe you're making a lot of assumptions about me."

"You told me you didn't want an affair."

"Can't a girl change her mind?" she asked before her lips settled over his.

GRAY WASN'T SURE HE heard her correctly. Or even if these past ten minutes were real. He'd only enjoyed two glasses of wine, hardly enough to make him hallucinate. Yet here he sat, a warm and willing Amy in his arms, and she'd just announced she'd changed her mind about their agreement. About having an affair.

He didn't want to think of making love with her as having an affair. Instinctively, he knew their joining would mean more than that convenient phrase. He could see it in her blue eyes, so warm and trusting, so filled with need and resolution.

"Are you sure?"

"Yes."

He needed no further clarification, no more encouragement to cover her lips with his and hold her tight. Her mouth tasted of fragrant coffee and desire, and he grew more intoxicated from the kiss than from the wine. She moaned deep in her throat, a sound that reverberated through both of them. His fingers plunged through her dark hair as he deepened the kiss.

A portion of his brain, the part that separated him from a raging beast, told him to slow down. To get in control. To charm and seduce with calculated moves and soft words. He fought for control as the primitive side of him struggled for dominance.

Amy wasn't helping. Her nails raked his chest through the thin sweater. She pressed her breasts against him, giving a soft whimper when his lips trailed from her mouth down her throat. He took a deep breath, causing a shudder to ripple through her. Strength, that was what he needed at the moment. She was driving him crazy with her uninhibited responses.

Somehow, he needed to get them upstairs to his bed. Soon, before he pressed her back into the cushions. Before he forgot everything but losing himself in Amy's willing warmth.

"Upstairs," he murmured against the soft skin before her ear.

"Now," she answered, pulling at his shoulders.

"I don't have any protection down here."

She moaned. "How are we going to get up the stairs? I can't stop kissing you. I want to feel your hands on me."

He swelled even harder. He felt ready to explode, but he pushed up from the couch with extreme effort. "Come here," he commanded.

Amy surged into his arms. His hands skimmed

down her back to cup her bottom. "Hold on," he said as he lifted her. Her arms fastened around his neck. He eased his hands lower, molding her thighs to his waist. With a moan of surrender, she locked her legs around him.

Walking wasn't easy with her moving against him, but somehow he managed to make it to the landing before stopping. Pressing her against the wall, he kissed her until they were both breathing hard and fast.

"Almost there," he whispered against her neck as he continued up the stairs. Light from the room below filtered into the loft, showing him the way to the bed. Almost there, in more ways than one, he thought as Amy took his earlobe into her mouth and sucked.

Fortunately, his king-size bed sported a high mattress. He eased Amy onto the soft comforter, then unwrapped her arms from around his neck and shoulders with a small sound of protest.

"Just for a moment, sweetheart," he said easily, wondering why he'd used that particular endearment. Not that this was the time to analyze anything, including his feelings....

She stretched, reaching up and to the side, pulling her white silky blouse tight against her breasts. Her legs, no longer hooked around his waist, still rested on either side of his knees. He longed to uncover all her secrets, but first he wanted to savor the sight of her, lying so provocatively against his dark linens. "You are so beautiful."

"You're looking awfully good yourself," she said, kicking off her shoes and running her stocking feet up his sides. "Why don't you join me down here?"

"If you insist." He pulled the cashmere sweater over his head and dropped it to the floor. Next came his shoes, which he kicked away. Then he eased his weight down on his rigid forearms, hovering above Amy so he could continue to look at her. He'd dreamed of her being here, in his bed, but assumed this was one wish that wouldn't be granted.

She ran her palms over his chest. "Oh, I insist," she said breathlessly.

Gray lowered the rest of the way, until his chest brushed against her tight nipples, until he could capture her lips with his. Her arms snaked around his back and she pressed him closer, until all his weight lay on her, on the bed.

"Make love to me," she whispered when they broke the kiss.

He needed no further encouragement. Rolling to his side, he concentrated on unbuttoning her blouse. On helping her remove first that garment, then her tight, clinging leggings. He buried a groan in the curve of her neck when he saw the blatantly sexy bra and panties she wore. The white lace contrasted to her pale olive-toned skin, and he saw her dark nipples peeking through.

Her shiver told him he'd accidentally uncovered a sensitive spot on her neck, so he paused to explore, his tongue tasting, his lips coaxing a moan from her. Her fingers clenched against his arm, his back, as she shivered.

"Cold?"

"Hot." She dragged his mouth back to hers and kissed him deeply. When that wasn't enough, she pushed him to his back and tackled his jeans. His very tight jeans.

"Careful, sweetheart," he cautioned as she popped the button and slid the zipper down.

"I'm a doctor, remember? I'm always careful, especially with someone in such an...agitated state," she said in a husky voice as she caressed him through his briefs. He closed his eyes at her tender yet insistent touch, but opened them again when she began tugging at his jeans.

He raised his hips and she had him undressed, except for his briefs, in a few seconds. "You're very good at this."

"You're a cooperative patient."

"Are we playing doctor?" he asked, amused that she could tease him even though they were both highly aroused. He reached up and unhooked the front clasp of her bra, easing the lacy off her round, perfect breasts. The dark nipples appeared almost painfully tight, so he reached up to soothe them with his mouth.

"Not like I've ever played before," she whispered.

The time for teasing ended. He rolled over until she was once again under him, kissed her until they were both breathless and pressed his arousal against that sexy piece of silk that covered her. And when that wasn't enough, he swept away his briefs and her panties, reached inside the nightstand drawer and prepared himself.

When he eased inside, he looked into her eyes, wanting to absorb every sensation. She surrounded him, pulling him deeper into her body and into her life. Her legs anchored him even as her rapt expression kept him captive. They lay there for a moment, as if they were both afraid to move, to shatter the magic. But then she clenched him tight and he began to move, and all was lost. All his doubts, all his reservations. There was only Amy, moving with him, calling his name, convulsing around him until he could no longer think, until every nerve ending in his body combined in that one place where they were joined. He twined his fingers with hers and let himself go with a moan ripped from his soul.

AMY AWOKE SLOWLY, stretching languorously in Gray's bed. A sheet covered her from toes to breasts, but beneath the covers she was quite naked. Quite satisfied, too.

She felt wonderful. Better than wonderful. The only thing missing to make the night perfect was the man who had made her feel this good.

Where was he?

The rustle of paper and the sound of footsteps on the stairs answered that question. Light from below drifted upstairs with the sounds. Pushing herself up on her elbows, she focused on the top landing. In just a few seconds, he appeared, carrying the large gift bag she'd brought with her and a smaller package. He wore the same jeans he'd had on earlier, but his feet and chest were bare. He looked so good. Nearly too good to be true.

She couldn't hide her smile when he sat on the bed. "What have you been up to?"

"I locked up for the night," he answered, leaning across the bed. His brief kiss, warmth and woodsy cologne stirred her senses. "And I decided we should exchange our gifts up here. I'm pretty certain I don't want you getting out of bed."

"I have to be at the clinic in the morning. We'll be booked solid with appointments."

"Then we'd better get started. I do want you to get some sleep tonight."

Amy glanced at the clock. She obviously hadn't slept long, because it was only a few minutes after ten o'clock. "Surely exchanging gifts won't take that long."

"No," he said, leaning over the bed until she flopped back against the pillows, "but I had something else in mind for later."

"Oh." She smiled, then pulled him down for another kiss. She loved kissing him, especially now, when she knew what could follow. When she knew how incredible they were together. She'd suspected as much all along, but tonight had confirmed her instincts. Gray was more than a pretend boyfriend, more than a social date.

He was now her lover. They were having an affair.

"First, gifts," he whispered against her neck.

"You're sure?"

"I want to get this out of the way so I can unwrap my other present."

"Me?"

Gray smiled. "Best Christmas gift I've ever received."

Chapter Nine

He sat up and switched on the bedside lamp before reaching for the smaller box. Amy marveled at the elegant black and gold giftwrap. "Looks expensive."

"It's not polite to ask."

"I'm just making an observation." She turned the box around, noticing a gold foil sticker on the bottom. "Did you get this in Dallas?"

Gray nodded. "I wanted to get something appropriate for you, but I didn't want anyone around here to tell you what I was buying."

Amy sat up, hooking the sheet under her arms as she reached for her gift to Gray. "I wanted to get something appropriate for you, too, but you're a hard...I mean a *difficult*...man to buy for."

Gray gave her a slight smile, one eyebrow raised. "I have simple tastes."

Amy placed her index finger along her pursed lips and frowned. "Where have I heard that before? Ah, yes, a cat food commercial. I think the punch line is, 'Only the best.'"

"Hmm. It's nice to know what you think of me."

She snatched the gift box from his hands. "I think

you're pretty terrific. Now, what did you get for me?"

She carefully opened the black and gold paper, then pulled out a jeweler's box. She recognized the store logo, and her heart beat faster. Surely he hadn't purchased some expensive piece of jewelry. Good gracious, she was expecting leather gloves or a silk scarf! Neither would fit in such a small box.

"I wasn't sure what to get, so I thought this would be appropriate for you."

For a pretend girlfriend? she wanted to ask. She eased the top off and pulled out the velvet box inside. Thank goodness it didn't appear to be a ring box. They were smaller, weren't they?

"Gray, are you sure about this?"

"It's a Christmas gift, Amy. Nothing more."

"Okay." She took a deep breath and opened the box. A beautifully crafted white gold caduceus, sparkling with tiny diamonds, glittered in the golden light of the bedside lamp.

"For the town doctor," he said with a smile, tipping the box toward him and looking at the pin nestled against the royal blue velvet.

Amy told herself to be relieved this was only a pin for a doctor, not a personal piece of jewelry—like a ring—for a girlfriend. At the same time, she realized her feelings were confused because of their lovemaking earlier. She felt so much closer to Gray, so much less like a pretend date and more like a real lover.

But even as a lover, she couldn't accept something like a ring. No, that would cause too many tongues to wag in town.

"It's beautiful," she said softly. "You shouldn't have, but I think it's beautiful and I'll wear it proudly."

"You can wear it as a necklace, too," he advised, showing her a clasp on the back. "Just run a chain through here."

"Okay." She placed a hand along his jaw, then leaned forward and kissed him sweetly. He'd just shown her another side of him, the part that enjoyed giving and sincerely wanted the receiver to be pleased. "Now, it's time for you to open my gift."

He reached for the bag, then carefully separated the many layers of tissue. "Are you sure there's something inside here?" he teased.

"Absolutely." She sat up and pulled the sheet higher. She supposed she should get dressed, but there hadn't been an appropriate time. Besides, it was kind of fun to sit in bed naked and open Christmas presents. Definitely a new experience.

He pulled out the framed watercolor-and-ink original. "Amy, this is wonderful. How did you arrange for it so quickly?"

"I have my connections," she said mysteriously. In truth, a high school student who had some artwork displayed in the bank lobby had jumped at the opportunity for a commissioned painting. He'd barely finished it during Christmas break. Fortunately, the watercolor had dried quickly so she could put it in the frame just in time for the holiday.

"This looks just like Grayson Industries, only with the landscape a little more complete."

"I told the artist to fill in any gaps as he saw fit."

"I'll have to plant some crepe myrtle at the corners. I think he had a great idea.'' Gray tilted the framed watercolor, smiling as he took in the details. ''This is such a thoughtful gift. Thank you,'' he said as he leaned toward her for another sweet kiss.

''I'm glad you like it.''

''Not at much as I like you.''

He pressed her back into the pillows, the gifts pushed aside. His hands framed her face, and his lips descended. Amy's heart raced as she anticipated what was to follow.

A horrible, shrill siren split the night.

Amy sat up, dislodging both Gray and the sheet. ''What's that?''

''Either the smoke or carbon monoxide detector. It's never gone off before.''

Gray leaped from the bed, pulling Amy along by the hand. ''We have to get out of here now.''

''But I'm naked!''

He tossed her his black cashmere sweater and pulled a blanket off the floor, where they'd pushed it earlier. She grabbed her panties as they hurried toward the steps.''

''Our gifts!'' She turned back to the bed and placed both items in the large gift bag. She wasn't about to let either one burn up, just in case there really was a fire. Or there might be an explosion. The idea that this beautiful house might be in danger shook her as much as the shrill alarm.

Gray grabbed the cordless phone on the way down the stairs. Hand in hand they ran from the house and out to the driveway.

Gray wrapped his arms around her shivering body. She'd pulled his cashmere sweater down to her thighs. He'd wrapped the blanket around them both since his chest and arms were exposed. Both their feet were bare, and the concrete was dry and cold. Despite his natural warmth and enticing smell, the situation was no fun.

Amy did a lot of dancing around and rubbing her feet together, but she didn't think it was working. They weren't in danger of frostbite or imminent hypothermia—it wasn't that cold outside—but they were darn uncomfortable. Although she knew they needed the emergency crews to address whatever problem was occurring in the house, she wasn't looking forward to facing them wearing bikini panties and Gray's sweater.

So much for keeping their intimate relationship a secret. She'd really hoped she didn't have to announce to the world that she was carrying on a hot and heavy affair with Gray. Life would have been so much simpler if they'd only been seen on social dates.

Despite their intimate position and the lack of clothing, tension that had nothing to do with sexual desire radiated from him. He was no doubt worried about his house, although he'd sworn he wasn't. They'd watched for any signs of fire. They'd also kept all the windows and doors closed, as instructed by 911, in case there was a leak.

"I still don't see any smoke," she said.

"I really think it was the carbon monoxide detector."

He'd told the dispatcher that, so perhaps they'd send someone beside the officer on duty and the volunteer fire department. Someone who could fix the problem. "You're probably right. Tug must have hooked up his gizmo or gadget or whatchamacallit wrong."

"I'm going to murder him."

"Not if I get to him first," she said through clenched, rattling teeth.

The sound of sirens drifted through the night. Headlights darted wildly as several vehicles wound their way through the hills to Gray's house. "I'm not ready for this," she said, hating the thin, reedy quality of her voice. Hating the thought that in about thirty seconds, Ranger Springs's arsenal of rescue personnel were ascending on them.

"You can take the blanket and..." he looked around, frowning at the sparse landscape with low bushes and no large trees.

And hide was what Gray meant. No matter how tempting the proposition, she didn't think it would help. For one thing, her locked car—Why in the world had she locked her car in this remote location?—was still parked in the circular drive. For another, someone was bound to spot her sooner or later, lurking in the bare-branch azaleas or peeking out from behind the low cedar bushes. How ridiculous would she look then?

"I'm not ashamed of what we did. I'm just sorry we got caught."

A black Bronco screeched to a halt beside Amy's car, the alternating red and blue lights flashing a wild kaleidoscope across the landscape.

Gray's expression seemed more grim. "At least Ethan showed up."

"This is good?"

"Better than some deputy or patrolman I don't know."

Gray pulled Amy behind him and adjusted the blanket as the fire truck pulled in back of the Bronco. More red lights flashed wildly, illuminating the night. Volunteer firemen, most as haphazardly dressed as she—except they wore pants and shoes—jumped off the truck. She knew most of them. Some were her patients; some had been in school with her. Some were just friends of the family.

All of them would be talking about this tomorrow.

With a sigh, she tugged the cashmere sweater farther down her thighs and said a silent prayer that she'd become as invisible.

Thankfully, the fireman got busy with equipment on their engine. Ethan Parker, Gray's friend and chief of police, walked over to them.

"I take it this was bad timing," he said to Gray, a slight smile on his face. He looked over Gray's shoulder. "Hello, Dr. Amy."

"Hello, Chief."

"Quit smirking," Gray remarked. "From where I'm standing, this isn't funny."

"Of course not. But from where I'm standing, just a tiny smirk seemed appropriate."

"You're enjoying this, aren't you?"

"Sure. My idea of fun is getting up in the middle of the night, leaving my nice warm bed and sweet wife, and coming out her to rescue your butt."

That seemed to silence Gray. His friendship with Ethan was one of the reasons he'd moved his business to Ranger Springs rather than some other small town. Although they didn't socialize often since

Ethan was now married, Amy knew the two men had a close relationship.

Ethan glanced at both of them. "Would you like to get in out of the cold? The Bronco's warm."

"You don't have to ask me twice," Amy said.

"I'm going to talk to Ethan for a moment."

Amy disengaged herself from Gray's very warm, very bare back. "Keep the blanket. I'll be fine inside the vehicle."

As quickly and unobtrusively as possible, she walked to the Bronco. Before she made it inside, another vehicle pulled to a screeching halt beside the fire truck, catching her in the high beams. "Hanson's Air Conditioning and Heating to the rescue," Amy murmured, knowing the night had just gotten worse.

"WELL, THAT WAS AN interesting evening," Gray said as he stood by the large window in the living room and watched the Hanson van roll away into the waning hours of the morning.

"It started out pretty good," Amy said, walking up behind him, sipping her third or fourth cup of hot tea.

He turned and tried to give her a reassuring smile. "That would be the meal, right? I hope what followed was more than 'pretty good.'"

"Fishing for compliments? Okay, it was great. I'm not sorry about what we did, but I had hoped to keep it between us. I'm not used to having my personal life discussed around every coffeepot and across every table."

Gray placed his hands on her upper arms. "Of course you are," he corrected gently. "They talk about you all the time, usually in a complimentary way. They want you to be happy. You're their collective daughter, their friend, their physician. The difference is now they have something a little more juicy to discuss."

"How encouraging. I wonder how long the 'juicy' topic will last."

"You're the expert on small towns, but from my observations, this should keep them talking for a good while."

Amy buried her face against his chest, her breath teasing him through the sweater he'd donned when they were allowed back in the house. "I really hate this. I don't want to look into my patients' faces and wonder if they're disappointed in me as a person. I don't want my father to endure snide remarks or sympathetic gestures over his daughter's immoral conduct."

Gray took the mug from her and put it on a nearby table. "Then there's only one thing we can do."

"I don't want to stop seeing you."

Her soft voice sent a shiver of anticipation through him. He wanted her to want him. After one night of making love, he couldn't consider letting her go. Not without a fight, especially when all they were battling were a few potentially narrow-minded opinions.

"Then agree to be my fiancée."

She pulled back, her blue eyes wide and startled. "What?"

He took a deep breath, knowing so much depended on his reasoning. "We're already pretending to be dating. How much more complicated will it be to take it another step? If the citizens of Ranger Springs believe we're getting married, surely they won't think too badly of us for doing more than sharing meals and attending parties together."

"But...you mean take our dating relationship to a greater height of deception?"

He frowned. "I wouldn't put it like that."

"It's exactly like that. I mean, we aren't getting married."

The words hung heavily in the air. He didn't want to think as far ahead as marriage. Engagement was enough for now. *Enough to keep her in his bed.* Even as the thought popped into his head, he knew he was being selfish and petty. He should be thinking of the larger issue: the problem of Amy's reputation and his position in the business community.

Yes, a pretend engagement was exactly what he and Amy needed to stabilize the situation. As long as everyone was happy, he and Amy could continue their relationship. They would be seen together in public, but in private, they could explore this strong attraction. Their sexual chemistry hadn't been unexpected based on their initial reaction to each other, but was startling nonetheless. He wouldn't give that up for any reason, especially one as flimsy as worry over what other people thought.

"Is a pretend engagement such a difference from a pretend dating situation?" he reasoned.

"Yes! If we tell everyone we're engaged, they'll actually expect us to get married!"

"I don't see any problem, Amy," he said calmly. "Lots of couples have long engagements." He placed one palm against her cheek, then sunk his fingers into her hair. "Maybe we'll enjoy being engaged more than we did just dating."

"But to what end?"

Gray shrugged. "Why don't we take it one day at a time."

ONE DAY AT A TIME? The man was obviously crazy, Amy thought as she tossed restlessly in her own bed. Maybe he'd breathed in too much carbon monoxide and his thinking was confused. Muddled. That was the only explanation for this plan of his to combat the talk that was sure to follow.

Ethan wouldn't say anything, but Tug would. And at least half of the volunteer fire department would have told their wives or girlfriends already. *You should have seen Dr. Amy, barefoot and wearing only that man's sweater!* She didn't need one of Gray's sophisticated hearing devices to hear the gossip.

But to pretend an engagement to avoid criticism? Could she do that? Should she do that? She'd be deceiving her father even more. He was already hoping Gray would be the right man for her. She felt terrible about getting his hopes up. Her father believed in happily-ever-after...until death do us part. Hadn't he waited eighteen years to date again after her mother's death?

Amy sighed, hugging her pillow to her chest. She hadn't been able to sleep, despite arriving home around three o'clock in the morning. She wanted to call her father, to ask him to cover her shift at the clinic in the morning, but her absence would no doubt make the rumors more dramatic. She could imagine the *Springs Gazette* lead story: *After a wild night of sex, Dr. Amy Wheatley called in sick at the medical clinic, ignoring her patients for her lover, prominent Ranger Springs businessman Grayson Phillips.*

This time she groaned and gave up on the idea of sleeping. She might as well make a pot of coffee, fix herself some breakfast and get over to the clinic early. She could get some paperwork done before Gladys arrived.

And she could think about her answer to Gray's proposition. He'd kissed her tenderly when she'd left his house, asking her to call him later with a response. She had no idea what she would say. She suspected she wasn't thinking too clearly.

Three hours later, bleary eyed from lack of sleep and an abundance of charts and forms, Amy looked up to see her father standing in the doorway.

"Good morning, Daddy," she said as cheerfully as possible.

"You look like hell, Amy girl."

"Thanks. It's good to see you too."

"You had a bit of excitement last night, I hear," he said, walking into her office and sitting in one of the chairs.

"Where did you hear that?" she asked carefully.

"Down at the café. Seems Jimmy Mack Branson's son was on the fire truck that made a late night call out to Gray's house. He told Jimmy Mack, who told Thelma while I was gettin' coffee this mornin'."

"Gray suspected the grapevine would be especially busy this morning."

"Well now, it's not everyday that a whole truckload of our friends and neighbors get to see my girl runnin' around barefoot in the middle of the night wearin' nothin' but a sweater."

Amy winced at her father's plain-spoken words. "At least the gossips got most of the details right." She'd definitely been barefoot, wearing little besides Gray's sweater. "I *was* wearing my panties, by the way."

"This situation doesn't sound too funny from this old man's point of view." Her father's face was getting red and he was frowning. She didn't want to be the cause of her father's unhappiness, but darn it, he shouldn't question her decision. She'd just been in the right place at the wrong time!

"It didn't seem real funny to us, either, when the alarm went off while we were opening presents."

"You had to undress to open your Christmas presents?"

No, we had to undress to have wild, uninhibited sex. "Daddy, you don't really want to know the details of last evening, do you? Because I'd like to remind you I'm a grown woman who has graduated from medical school and lived on my own in the big city."

"This isn't some big city. It's a small town, and it looks darn fishy when the town's doctor is runnin' around in her underpants in the middle of the night with some man who's not her husband."

"Well, maybe he's going to be my husband!"

Her father's scowl brightened. He sat up straighter in the chair. "What did you say?"

She took a deep breath. Now that she'd blurted out the only thing that would silence his lecture, she wondered why she wasn't panicking. Why she didn't want to immediately call back the words. She'd practically admitted they were engaged and all she felt was relief that her father wasn't treating her like a seventeen year old on prom night.

"I said we might be getting engaged."

"Might be? Did he or did he not propose?"

"He...proposed." Proposed an engagement, that is.

"So, what did you say?"

"I said I was going to have a really busy day, and I'd have to get back to him."

"What!"

Gladys stuck her head into the office. "First patients are coming in."

"What did I tell you, Daddy? We'll have to talk about this later."

He drew his gray eyebrows together and scowled at her for a long moment. Finally, he pushed out of the chair and limped to the door. He turned back and said, "Are you talkin' to him soon?"

"I'm sure I will, Daddy." If Gray proved true to form, he'd show up at the clinic before the day was finished, warm promises in his pewter eyes, coaxing words on his sculpted lips. Oh, yes. She'd be talking to him soon.

Chapter Ten

Gray briefly considered traveling to Dallas for another purchase at the prestigious jewelry store where he'd bought Amy's Christmas present, but nixed the idea. He didn't want to abandon her during the holiday period, especially when she'd be hearing all the gossip. Besides, since he was trying to impress the citizens of Ranger Springs with what a nice guy he was, he'd better give the local jeweler his business.

There was no way this purchase would remain a secret for long.

Like many of the businesses in town, the jewelry store's door was equipped with a tinkling bell that announced customers. "Hello, Mr. Phillips," the gray-haired man behind the counter greeted him. "What can we do for you today?"

"I need a ring, Mr...."

"Schuler. For yourself?"

"No," Gray said, wandering over to the bridal sets. "This one will be for a very special lady."

"Really!" Dollar signs seemed to dance in Mr. Schuler's dark eyes. "Well, you've come to the right place."

Twenty minutes later, Gray exited the store after many smiles and much hand-pumping. The jeweler assured him that the ring would be ready by Friday.

Amy hadn't exactly given him an answer yet, but he was going to be prepared. Next time he asked to become engaged, he'd be better prepared. More romantic. She deserved that much from a fiancé, he believed, even one she might consider temporary.

"AMY AND GRAY ARE GETTIN' married," Ambrose said as he sat down for lunch with Thelma and Joyce. Patients had been plentiful, but he'd convinced Amy they should take a break and not try to work in additional cases unless they were emergencies. She needed a nap, and he needed to break the news to his matchmaking cronies.

Joyce beamed. "See, I told you our plan would work! We just had to keep pushing them together during the holidays."

"Well, I do believe they were about as together as a couple could get last night," Thelma observed. She was probably still a bit peeved no one had gotten a photo of the emergency vehicles at Gray's house for the paper. Ambrose was thankful no one had snapped a picture.

"How do you know for sure?" Joyce asked, her manicured hand on his arm bringing him out of those dark thoughts. She sure wore pretty polish. Today it was a sparkling red to go with her Christmas outfits.

"Amy told me this morning. She said something about Gray was going to be her husband, and I asked her if that meant he'd proposed, and she said she told him she'd get back to him. But she wouldn't have mentioned the husband part if she wasn't going to say 'yes' when she gets back to him."

"Hmm," Joyce said. "Were you two having an argument at the time?"

"No! Well, sort of. Not really an argument, but a discussion of how it looked for the town doctor to be foolin' around in the middle of the night out at Gray's house."

"Maybe she just told you that to get you off her case," Thelma offered.

"I don't think so."

"You certainly don't want to think so, but it's a possibility," Joyce added.

Ambrose shook his head. "My Amy's gettin' married, and that's the end of it."

"I HEARD SOME INTERESTING news when I stopped by the Kash 'n' Karry," Helen Kaminsky said. She'd brought Matthew in for a checkup after his appendectomy. Apparently Helen was baby-sitting while his mother was working extra hours during the holidays.

"Does that hurt?" Amy asked, pressing gently on the boy's side.

"No, ma'am."

"Good."

"Jimmy Mack Branson's store is right across the square from Schuler's Jewelry store, and he said Mr. Schuler had an interesting customer in first thing this morning."

"Really?" Amy feigned disinterest, but she couldn't tell if she dreaded hearing this latest news, or if she welcomed the gossip that told her what Gray was up to.

And she was certain Helen was talking about Gray. That's all anyone had talked about all day. Between sneezes, sniffles and pulled backs, she'd given lots of updates on the state of his heating system.

"That's right. Gray drove up to the store in that luxury car of his and made a special purchase."

"How do you know what he bought?"

"Because Jimmy Mack went over to see Mr. Schuler during lunch, and he said he had to get his diamond broker on the phone to find just the perfect stone."

Amy stared at the neat stitches in Matthew's abdomen. The surgeon had done a good job. And what was she supposed to say about Gray's diamond purchase? She didn't even know how she felt about getting engaged!

"Dr. Amy, did you hear me? Gray bought a *diamond* from Schuler's Jewelry!"

"Helen," Amy said, placing her palm over the older lady's hand, "I know this all seems so exciting, what with the scare we had over the carbon monoxide detector, and the fire department, and...everything, but believe me, wedding announcements are premature."

Helen sighed. "You and Gray make such a nice couple."

Amy smiled, turning her attention back to her patient. "Get dressed now, cowboy. You're almost as good as new."

"Great!"

Now if she could only fix all this gossip.

The rest of the day went by quickly, with appointments until after five-thirty. Even Mr. Gresham came in—with his wife—for a blood pressure checkup. By the time Amy got home, she was bushed.

Gray called that evening while she was curled up on her bed sorting towels from underwear after she'd done a load of laundry. "How was your day?"

"Filled with questions. And yours?"

"Filled with speculative looks."

She tucked the phone between her shoulder and ear and settled against the headboard. "Sounds like you got the better end of this deal."

"Hey, I'm the one with the defective furnace."

Amy smiled. "It's fixed, and I don't think that's what those looks were about."

She heard Gray chuckle. "I take it you weren't quizzed on whether the volunteer fire department provides good emergency service."

"You've got that one right."

His chuckle faded away to silence before he said, "I missed you today."

"I thought about you, too." She didn't know what else to say.

"I want to see you again."

She paused, torn between telling him how badly she wanted to drive to his house and how she needed time to decide her feelings about their changing relationship. "I'm going to be busy at the clinic. We always have a lot of kids in during the holiday breaks."

Silence stretched tight for a few moments, then he said, "Then have dinner with me on Friday."

She took a deep breath. "Okay."

"How about the German restaurant in Wimberley? Or would you like to go into the city? We could spend the weekend in San Antonio."

"I...I'd better not be gone on Saturday. We're going to have the clinic open a half day." She also wasn't sure how she felt about spending the night with him. Would that mean they were having an affair? A real affair? Or would he expect to make love because he assumed they were getting engaged?

"I'll be at your place Friday around seven o'clock then," Gray said, his voice growing softer, sexier, as he spoke. "I'm looking forward to seeing you again."

"Me, too," Amy said with a sigh. "Good night."

She'd thought this relationship was going to be easy, but it wasn't. She had a feeling it would get more confusing before she figured out whether she was going to say yes or no—and to what question.

IF SHE DIDN'T KNOW BETTER, she'd swear someone was using Gray's listening devices to bug her phone. There seemed to be too many Ranger Springs residents at the restaurant to be coincidence. As she and Gray walked to their table in the back of the room, she passed Ralph Biggerstaff and his wife, who greeted them with smiles. A few tables away, Ethan Parker and his wife, Robin, were enjoying salads. Ethan stood up, shook Gray's hand, and nodded to Amy. Robin said hello to them both before their attention was captured by another couple. Ambrose Wheatley and Joyce sat near the fireplace, already well into their meal.

''Daddy, you didn't mention you were coming here tonight.'' She smiled at his dinner companion. ''Good evening, Joyce.''

''Hello, Amy. Hi, Gray.''

''Neither did you,'' Ambrose said. He nodded at Gray. ''How are things going, son?''

Amy closed her eyes. Son. Why didn't he just announce his preferences to the world? Her father rarely called anyone over the age of ten ''son.'' She wanted to look around and see if her neighbors were watching or listening, but that would be too obvious.

''I'm fine, Dr. Wheatley. And yourself?''

''Gettin' along better now that the leg's almost well.''

''We'd better get to our table, Daddy,'' Amy said, interrupting the male bonding.

''You two have a nice dinner now,'' her father said.

''Scc you soon,'' Joyce added.

Finally, they were seated at a table in an alcove by a leaded glass window. The night sky reflected the warm colors and candlelight inside the restaurant.

They ordered a favorite Riesling wine, but declined an appetizer. Amy doubted that she'd be able to swallow any solid food, even though the tantalizing smells wafting through the darkened room were some of her favorites. She felt the eyes of the world on her, despite the private table and quiet conversations going on around them.

''You're awfully quiet tonight,'' Gray commented.

''This is a little uncomfortable.'' She looked around the room. ''I feel like everyone is watching and listening, even though this table is fairly private and I can see others talking.'' She shrugged, the feeling still with her. ''I suppose I'm a little paranoid, hmm?''

''Are you sure it's not me that you're uncomfortable with?''

''No!'' she said quickly.

''Because you've barely looked at me all evening.''

''Sure I have.'' She picked up her wineglass and twirled the pale liquid, watching the candlelight play off the ripples.

''What am I wearing?''

Her head raised and she looked at him.

''No cheating. Just tell me what you remember.''

Amy closed her eyes, trying to bring up the image of Gray. Intense silver eyes, lean sculpted cheeks, sensuous lips. And his body, as golden as his eyes were silver, so hard and lean and warm that her insides clenched and shivered. She wanted to know more about him, what he liked and disliked, where he was most sensitive, and how she could drive him wild. Yes, driving Gray wild had definite appeal. She'd never felt such strong desire before.

''Amy,'' he chided, ''I don't think you're paying attention.''

She opened her eyes, suddenly realizing she was breathing fast and her face was flushed. ''You're right,'' she admitted. ''I wasn't exactly thinking about what you're wearing tonight.''

He leaned closer, his voice barely a whisper. ''Were you thinking about Tuesday night?''

She swallowed. ''Yes.''

"If you keep looking at me like that, I'm going to carry you off without any dinner."

"As a doctor, I'd advise against taking a rash action. For one thing, you need to keep your strength up. For another, this restaurant is full of people who'd love something new to talk about."

"Are they already bored with Tuesday night's activities?"

"Not quite." *I certainly wasn't bored. I'm not bored now,* she wanted to say. Making love with Gray had been so special, so intense, that she didn't have words to express her feelings. The experience transcended her previous encounters.

The waiter came and took their order. When he left, Gray leaned forward again, his eyes sparkling. "When you said I needed to keep my strength up, were you talking about later?"

"Maybe. I don't know. I'm as confused as most of the people who keep asking me about...us."

Amy barely remembered what they ate. Her mind kept wandering to dessert. Gray, stretched on the soft cotton sheets of his king-size bed. Or reclining on the lacy pillows against her headboard. All delicious options, and all nonfattening.

"Let's have some coffee," he said. She wondered why he was dawdling when all she wanted to do was drag him home. Either house would be fine. Heck, the Lexus was pretty spacious.

She closed her eyes, reminding herself that she was a grown woman, a professional, and had to act the part. She *could* be patient. "Okay."

The waiter cleared the table quickly and efficiently, then set two cups of coffee on the table. She thought of the rumors she'd heard. Maybe Gray had bought a ring. Amy stirred cream into the cup. Maybe he was going to ask her to pretend to be engaged to him at the New Year's Eve party they were attending on Sunday.

She looked up to see a ring box from Schuler's Jewelry on the table in front of Gray.

She swallowed. Maybe he was going to ask her tonight.

"Amy," he said, reaching for her hand. Her heart raced so fast she imagined he'd be able to see the rapid thump-thump-thump through the chenille sweater she wore. "I know I asked you this question the other night, but I'd like to do it more…well, just better this time."

He swallowed, looking a little nervous himself, which was ridiculous, because this was only a pretend engagement. The ring might be real, but the engagement would be a deception. He opened the box, lifting a large emerald-cut diamond ring in white gold out of the velvet box.

"Would you do me the honor of accepting this ring?"

He hadn't asked her to be his wife, only to accept this ring. She supposed she could do that. After all, the whole town was expecting the engagement. He'd already bought the diamond from Mr. Schuler.

"This is a beautiful ring," she said, then realized the inanity of the comment. Where were the warm feelings of love and commitment? How could she wear this gorgeous ring for months and not get attached to both it and the man who gave it to her? Temporarily, she reminded herself.

Her heart rate slowed as reality sank in. She wasn't really going to marry Gray. She was just going to be his fiancée for a while. Until they grew tired of each other, or found someone else, or the town grew bored with gossip about them.

She inched her hand across the table, her fingers trembling. She shouldn't be trembling. She should be steady and sure because this action was necessary. At least, Gray believed it was necessary.

"Yes," she whispered. "I'll accept your ring." For now.

He looked into her eyes, his own troubled.

"It's okay," she assured him. "This is the right thing to do."

"This feels very right to me."

"This is like a fairy tale," she said softly, breaking eye contact. It wasn't any more real than the stories her mother had read to her when she was a child.

He slid the ring onto her finger. It fit perfectly. Mr. Schuler must have kept her size on file from when her father bought her a pearl ring for college graduation, she thought vaguely. Why was Gray doing this? Why tonight, why here?

Tears came to her eyes as she looked at her hand, the diamond sparkling wildly in the candlelight. So beautiful, so permanent in appearances. Gray cradled her hand, holding her firmly. She felt like crying.

When she looked up again, she saw his face like the facets of the diamond, distorted by her tears. And then the faces of the other diners, including her father and Joyce, Ralph and his wife and the rest of the Ranger Springs crowd who were here tonight. First one, then more, began to stand and clap until all of the restaurant shared in the moment.

She truly felt like crying.

Gray reached across the table and dabbed her tears away with his cloth napkin. "Don't cry, sweetheart."

"I can't help it."

"Tell me why."

She shook her head, attempting a smile. "Maybe sometime."

The clapping faded as she faced the restaurant. Gray took her hand in his, linked their fingers, and smiled for the crowd. "She said yes."

Amy closed her eyes so she wouldn't see the smiling faces of all the people they were deceiving. The one with the biggest grin was her dad.

Chapter Eleven

To prepare for tonight's New Year's Eve party, Amy settled her plum jersey dress over her head, let it slide down her hips and then zipped it up in back. The dress was plain, but hugged her body in all the right places. Since the party tonight wasn't formal, she'd dressed for comfort. The tight sleeve caught on her newest piece of jewelry.

She'd been wearing Gray's ring for almost forty-eight hours, Amy thought as she stared at the sparkling emerald-cut diamond. Already she felt as if she'd been engaged forever. With a sigh, she wiggled the dress into place before making sure no loose threads were caught in the mounting.

She hadn't handled the situation very well on Friday night, she admitted as she slipped on her strappy sandals. For one thing, she'd been surprised. She wasn't good with the unexpected. Once, at the Fort Worth clinic, her colleagues had thrown a small surprise birthday party. She hadn't known what to say. Instead of enjoying cake and ice cream, she'd thought about her waiting patients and piles of paperwork. No, surprises weren't a favorite.

Although she had to admit Gray had handled "popping the question" rather well. She'd found out later that he hadn't invited all the Ranger Springs residents. They'd found out he was taking her to the restaurant from Ethan, who'd let it slip to his daytime dispatcher, Susie. They'd come out of curiosity and love, so she couldn't be too critical of their participation in her engagement. They'd assumed her tears were those of joy, not of fear and confusion.

She pinned the diamond-encrusted caduceus onto the bodice of her dress, admiring the workmanship and detail. Gray certainly had a good eye for jewelry. Her engagement ring sparkled in the lights of the vanity. She paused once more to admire it, resting her hand against the dark fabric of her dress. He'd really picked out a beauty. She was going to miss this ring.

When they were no longer engaged, she hoped he could get his money back on the diamond. Or at least use it in another mounting—maybe for himself. After all, he'd vowed never to marry again, and she believed him. He held a part of himself back, as if he was afraid he might fall in love if he let his guard down. She knew he was attracted to her, but she didn't presume that she *could* make him fall in love with her, even if she wanted him to. Her previous experience with men, from boys in high school throughout professionals in her medical career, had proved that attractions were fleeting. The kind of love that had true staying power was rare, something she'd never experienced except inside the family with her father and mother.

She had a strong suspicion she could fall hard for

Gray, if only he'd open himself up a little. And that knowledge frightened her. She didn't want to fall in love with a man who wouldn't love her in return. She never wanted to make someone love her.

GRAY HAD BEEN TO THE country club in Dripping Springs several times in the past, but he'd never enjoyed a social function as much as he was this New Year's Eve party. The difference existed in the woman beside him, the woman who wore his ring. A fierce sense of joy swept through him whenever he saw that diamond on Amy's finger.

Not that *she* belonged to him. Never that. But she had accepted his ring, the one he'd chosen to make a statement to the world. *She's mine.* The feeling was unexpected. What had begun as a way to avoid unwanted dates had turned into so much more. He wasn't sure in what direction the relationship was going, but to something beyond convenience. Something beyond pretending to be involved for the sake of others.

"Having fun?" she asked him, bringing his attention back to the present. She looked beautiful tonight with her dark hair swept up in some sort of clip, strands teasing her neckline. The dress she wore fit perfectly, showing her curves and graceful posture. The pin he'd given her for Christmas was the only jewelry she wore except for some small sparkling earrings and the engagement ring.

Maybe for Valentine's Day he'd get her some diamond earrings to match the ring. They'd look beautiful on her delicate ears. He smiled at her, wishing they were someplace private. ‘‘Only because you’re with me.’’

‘‘What a nice answer! I wish I knew if it were true.’’

‘‘What do you mean?’’

‘‘Sometimes you’re so perfect I can’t decide if you’re real.’’

Her answer angered him. Quick, hot anger that swept through his body. He had the irrational urge to show her how imperfect he could be by pulling her into his arms and kissing her senseless, right here in the elegant country club ballroom. He wanted to run his fingers through her hair, press his body against her, take her—

‘‘Gray?’’

He took a deep breath. ‘‘What?’’

‘‘You looked…strange. What’s wrong?’’

‘‘I’m just a little upset that you seem to believe I’m lying to you.’’

She appeared shocked. ‘‘I never accused you of lying!’’

‘‘You said I was too perfect to be real.’’

‘‘That was a compliment.’’

‘‘It sounded like an insult.’’

She narrowed her eyes. ‘‘Are we having our first argument as an engaged couple?’’

‘‘I suppose we are.’’ He took another deep breath, then leaned closer. ‘‘I have an irrational urge to kiss you—hard, not one of those easy, slow kisses. And I’d like to stretch you out on that buffet table, right between the little cheesecake squares and the strawberries with whipped cream. I’m using all my concentration to keep from acting on my impulses, because the logical part of my brain knows that you would not appreciate being treated like dessert."

She smiled, her lips turning up in a secretive, seductive way that made his fingers clench tighter around the glass of single malt Scotch he'd been sipping all night. "Funny you should mention dessert. The other night, at the German restaurant in Wimberley..."

"Go on."

"Right before you gave me the ring," she said, flashing a smile and the diamond, giving him another fierce surge of pride, "I had a similar vision. I was thinking that you—"

"Amy! How wonderful to see you again."

The strident voice cut through the wonderful fantasy she'd begun to weave. He turned to see who had so inconveniently interrupted them.

"Maryanne," Amy said with feigned enthusiasm. He'd been around her enough to recognize that polite tone of voice she used when she had to say the appropriate words.

"I just noticed you across the room." As she'd done at the medical fund-raiser in Austin, Maryanne hugged Amy politely and placed an air kiss near her temple. "How wonderful you look tonight."

As if she didn't always look great. He smiled politely.

"If I'm not mistaken, this handsome man was also your date at the charity event a few months ago."

"That's right," Amy said, giving him a mischievous look as she placed her left hand on his arm. "Maryanne Perkins Bridges, may I present my fiancé, Grayson Phillips?"

AMY FELT A STRONG SURGE of pride when she introduced Gray to Maryanne again, this time as her fiancé. She watched her former rival closely, detecting a bit of jealousy as Maryanne's gaze roamed over Gray's well-tailored charcoal suit, his precisely cut hair and his handsome features.

He did appear almost too good to be true, but she wasn't going to accuse him of deceiving her again. She hadn't meant the remark that way, but she had spoken without thinking. Gray wasn't a naturally deceptive person, she sensed, even though he was a deliberately private one.

If they were really getting married, she'd expect him to be more open. Since they weren't...

"Engaged!" Maryanne shrieked. "How marvelous. When did all this happen?"

"Friday night," Amy answered. Gray put his arm around her and smiled at Maryanne.

"Why, you're only just engaged. And so soon."

"I feel like I've known Amy forever," Gray said. "Being without her another moment was out of the question."

"How romantic," Maryanne sighed. Her distinguished-looking husband approached them, his hand coming to rest on her shoulder.

"Darling," he said, "introduce me to your friends."

Amy recognized Weldon Bridges, the much older doctor Maryanne had married several years ago, but he obviously didn't remember her. While still a striking man, he and Maryanne looked more like father and daughter than husband and wife. Apparently

Hollywood didn't have a monopoly on these May/December relationships.

They chatted about the party, the weather and the traffic for a few minutes before Maryanne directed her attention back to Amy. "How is the medical clinic in Ranger Springs?"

"Just fine, thank you. I'm enjoying being back home."

"Still, it's sometimes difficult to compete against the larger clinic in the cities, especially the ones with more technology."

"I'm planning on updating the equipment very soon."

"Really? Well, that's admirable. Tell me," she said, taking a sip of champagne, "have you ever thought of selling to a corporation who could provide that type of technology?"

Selling? No, the thought had never crossed her mind. The Wheatley Medical Clinic needed to be independent. A Wheatley should be the physician, not some stranger who didn't know the community.

"No, Maryanne, I know I can speak for my father when I say we're not interested in selling." She wanted the clinic to go on for a long, long time, even after her father retired. She wanted life in Ranger Springs to continue uninterrupted, even with friends who meddled in your life and patients who questioned your qualifications.

She'd just gotten her life settled—or as settled as possible, given the situation with Gray—and she didn't want anything to disrupt it. Perhaps she was too young to be considered a stick-in-the-mud, but where her personal and professional lives were concerned, she didn't want change. She needed stability more than excitement, more than wealth.

"What a shame. My husband and I are creating a chain of clinics in smaller towns. We'd love to consider yours as a candidate."

"Sorry, I'm not interested."

"It's nearly midnight, sweetheart," Gray said, leaning close to her ear. He smiled at Maryanne and her husband. "I'd like to spend the first moment of the new year alone with Amy. I'm sure you understand."

Maryanne sighed, clearly displeased by either her response or by Gray's artful excuse for them to leave. She was also staring at him with an appreciative gleam in her eyes.

"Nice to meet you, Dr. Bridges," Gray said.

"Yes, nice to see you both again," Amy added as Gray looped her arm through his.

Within moments he'd snared two glasses of champagne and steered her into a corner, behind a potted palm. "I don't want to risk getting sidetracked by any other acquaintances."

"Thank you," she said, taking a drink of champagne. "I certainly didn't want to talk to Maryanne and her husband any longer. What made her think we'd ever sell the clinic?"

"Probably greed on their part. I'm sure she hadn't really thought about how you feel about it."

Gray rubbed her shoulder. "Don't worry about her."

"I'm not. She just irritates me."

"Let's not start the new year thinking about Maryanne." He took both glasses and set them in the potted palm. Then his arms came around her and he pulled her closer.

"What should we be thinking of?"

"How about us?"

Her heart skipped a beat. "I thought 'we' are all settled for the moment."

"I don't feel settled."

"Why?"

"Because I want you so much. I can't stop thinking about last week. About Tuesday night."

"Your furnace?" she said weakly, trying to lighten the moment.

"Your body. Your passion," he whispered in her ear. "I can't stop thinking about you."

Her pulse pounded fast and hard. "What are we going to do about it?"

"Spend the night with me. Tonight. Let's go someplace private where no one will interrupt us, where no one will carry tales back to the café."

The band began to play and the countdown to the new year began. A new start, with new opportunities. She rested her left hand on his chest, the diamond sparkling even in the low light. "Yes."

"Three-two-one," Gray whispered. "Happy New Year." And then he kissed her, masterfully, thoroughly and passionately. Her arms crept around his neck and she put everything into kissing him back, showing him how very special he was to her. How much she wanted to be alone with him.

"Happy New Year to you, too," she said softly when the kiss ended, as cheers celebrating the new year faded away, as the band played "Auld Lang Syne." "Now, where was that hotel room?"

INSTEAD OF HEADING INTO Austin, Gray drove to a new chain hotel on nearby Highway 290. Amy felt pleasantly surprised that he'd spend New Year's in something less than plush. Gray always seemed so far above the norm, as though he wasn't part of the regular world. Just another indication of how strong an image he presented.

"I made a reservation earlier," he explained, "just in case." When he reached into the back seat of the Lexus and pulled out a gym bag, Amy raised her eyebrow.

Gray shrugged. "I wanted to be prepared. I didn't think you had a toothbrush and deodorant in that little purse of yours."

Amy shook her head and smiled. "No, I didn't, but to tell you the truth, the morning after is the last thing on my mind."

He parked in front of the room, then opened the lock with one hand while he kept the other arm around her shoulders. "I don't want to let you go," he said as he pushed the door open.

"I'm not going anywhere," she said, turning in his arms as the door shut, "except into that bed."

"Not yet."

He eased both hands into her hair, loosening the strands with his fingers. The clip that held the loose curls fell to the carpet. "I've been wanting to do that all night."

She closed her eyes as he massaged her scalp. When his lips touched hers, she was surprised for an instant, but then gave into the sensation of his warm, firm mouth. The stroke of his tongue. The seal of his lips over hers. She matched his passion, giving back equally until they were both breathing hard, their bodies trembling.

Gray looked deeply into her eyes as his fingers found the zipper of her dress, sliding it down until cool air touched her back. She shivered, moving even closer against the wall of Gray's chest. He was solid and warm, hard where she was soft, a perfect fit.

A temporary fit. No, she didn't want to go there tonight. Especially not now, when his hands were moving on her flesh, searching, seeking.

"Wait," she whispered. She pulled away, ready to be out of this clinging dress, ready to show Gray what she'd worn beneath. She tugged her sleeves down, exposing her shoulders, then the top of her breasts. The dress caught, so she hooked her fingers in the bodice and pulled it lower, past the lace of the strapless bustier.

"You're driving me crazy," Gray said through tense lips.

"I'm trying my best." She wiggled the dress lower, over her hips, until she stood before him in the raciest underwear she'd ever worn.

"Where did you get that outfit?"

"This old thing?" she asked, running her index finger along the top edge, from the swell of her breast to her exaggerated cleavage. "Mail order."

"I didn't know Ranger Springs allowed X-rated catalogs."

"It came in a brown-paper wrapper," she teased. "Actually, this is pretty tame. I could have gotten something even naughtier."

"Not if you want me to live."

"Remember," she said, "I know CPR."

"To hell with the bed," Gray said, reaching for the bare strip of skin above the lacy bikini panties, "the dresser is closer."

She laughed, feeling joyous and free. Free to make love to him. Free to show him how she felt, with her body if not with the words clogging her throat.

"Oh, no. The first time was fantastic, but we were wild for each other. I let you set the pace. This time I'm taking charge."

He pulled her against his arousal, pressing hard against her so she couldn't misunderstand the urgency in his eyes. "Take charge fast. I'm still wild for you."

"Where's your legendary self-control?" she asked as she loosened his tie, pulling it free. With a smile she hoped was both teasing and seductive, she began unfastening the buttons of his white shirt, revealing his firm chest inch by enticing inch.

"When I get you alone, I don't seem to have much."

"Hmm. Interesting," she said, running her hands up his abdomen and chest. He sucked in his breath, his muscles rippling with the effort, and then shuddered when she lightly scraped her nails across his flat nipples. "What do you think that means?"

"Enough talking," he growled, grabbing her hips and pulling her close. "I've decided you can take charge the second time."

"Do you always get what you want?" she asked, her lips just a fraction of an inch from his.

"Always." He kissed her fiercely, as though he could draw her into his soul. His tongue coaxed and demanded, and she complied, molding herself to him, reveling in the firm grip of his hands, the insistent press of his arousal. When he pulled her closer, her nipples rubbed against the lace of her bustier, pushing her desire higher.

Her fingers worked first the belt, then the button and zipper of his slacks as he walked her backward toward the bed. Despite vowing that he wasn't going to let her take charge, he moved back so she could run her hands around his waist, beneath the elastic of his briefs. When she moved her hands to his shoulders and pressed him onto the bed, he sat down.

"What are you doing?"

"Getting you naked."

He smiled tightly as she knelt, removing his shoes and socks.

She grasped his slacks and pulled them down his legs. Then she eased along the length of his body, reveling in the feeling of skin against skin, of the tight lace of her bustier and the soft cotton of his briefs. They kissed, breathless, moaning, until she felt his hands on her back.

"As great as you look in this, I'm ready to see you out of it."

His fingers were as nimble as any surgeons as he worked the hooks free. Amy breathed a sigh as he peeled the confining garment away from her. Her breasts brushed his chest, making him groan. She smiled.

Within seconds, he'd peeled away her lacy bikini panties and his briefs, and all teasing stopped. He kissed her deeply, rolling over until she was beneath him. His mouth found first one nipple, then the other, suckling hard until she writhed and held his head to her breasts. He overwhelmed her with passion, his hands and lips coaxing her to lose control. She did, moaning into his mouth, grasping him, pulling him into her warmth.

"Wait," he growled. He reached for his slacks, found a packet in his pocket, and tore it open with his teeth. Within seconds he was ready. He looked into her eyes as he pushed into her body. Their sighs mingled as he braced himself above her.

"Amy," he whispered.

She placed a finger against his lips, then closed her eyes as they began to move.

"Look at me."

She opened her eyes, her lids heavy as she gazed deeply into his dark eyes. Her muscles clenched inside, holding him tight as he moved deliberately, driving her higher and higher. He rolled his hips and she moaned, her nails pressing into his back. The sensations overwhelmed her, pushing aside any thoughts except the incredible way Gray, only Gray, made her feel. Her release rolled through her as she lost focus on his face, as darkness threatened.

She barely heard his answering groan, but she felt his completion, the heavy tenseness in his body before he relaxed upon her. His weight felt glorious. She held him as tightly as her weak arms would allow, just in case he had any thoughts of leaving her.

They lay joined for a long time, his hands gently brushing aside her damp hair, stroking the chill bumps on her arms where the cool air touched her. When he did move, it was to roll them beneath the covers, tucked tight together, until sleep claimed them both.

Chapter Twelve

The second time was slower, richer, but equally intense. In the aftermath of making love, sometime in the wee hours of the morning on New Year's Day, Gray lay in the king-size bed and decided he wanted to actually marry Amy, not just pretend to be engaged to her.

"Let's make it real," he whispered against her tousled hair.

"Mmm," she responded drowsily.

He smiled. He'd just proposed—something he'd vowed never to do again—and Amy was sound asleep. Well, he couldn't blame her. They'd exhausted each other. The only reason he was awake was because he couldn't stop thinking about her.

As he lay with her in his arms, her steady breathing ticking his chest, he recognized the sense of rightness he felt when he was with her. While their passion was explosive, their companionship was quieter, more steady. He liked that. He enjoyed being around her—in private, in public, and under all situations they'd experienced.

Amy wasn't like other women he'd known. He'd

accepted that fact early on, but hadn't really thought about how important her unique qualities would become. How much he'd miss her if she weren't in his life.

She stirred, her hand drifting across his chest, her leg hooking over his. He felt every glorious naked inch of her along his side, draped across his chest, and he wanted her again.

But not before they talked.

''Amy, sweetheart, are you awake?''

''No,'' she mumbled against his chest, sending chill bumps across his skin. Then her lips moved against him, tasting, kissing, and the chill turned to heat.

''Not before we talk,'' he said aloud this time.

''Talk?''

''That's right.''

''Is it morning?''

''No. Well, it's very early.'' He looked at the red numbers of the clock beside the bed. ''Almost three o'clock.''

Her hand strayed lower on his abdomen. His body sprang to attention.

''Why do we need to talk at three o'clock in the morning?'' she asked.

''Because I want us to get married. Really married.''

That got her attention. ''What?''

''I want to marry you. For real. I don't want to just be engaged temporarily.''

She pulled away from him, pushing her hair out of her face with one hand. ''You said you didn't want to get married again.''

He shrugged. "I didn't think I did. I've reconsidered."

"Why?"

This would be the tricky part. He knew women wanted to hear the reason their man wanted to marry them was because of undying love. Mad, passionate love that made logical thinking impossible. Crazy urges that turned sensible men into blabbering idiots. He couldn't lie to Amy. He'd been madly in love once; it wasn't an experience he was willing to repeat.

"Because," he began carefully, "we are really great together. I enjoy being around you, and I think you feel the same about me. We obviously have passion working for us. The whole town is thrilled that we're engaged."

"But...marriage?" She pulled the sheet up with her as she leaned against the headboard. In the room's dim light, he could see a combination of surprise, denial and something else. Maybe...hope?

"Why not? We have a lot in common."

"We have a lot of differences."

He sat up, feeling at a disadvantage lying on the bed, on linens that still smelled of their lovemaking. Grabbing the edge of the sheet to cover his lap, he sat cross-legged facing Amy. "We both love living in a small town."

"You put your business first."

"Yes, just as you need to put your patients first. Responsibility is important to both of us."

"You had a bad first marriage."

He shrugged. "I had unrealistic expectations about marriage, having never seen a successful one."

"Then why do it again?"

"I'm not as clueless now," he stated. "I've learned a lot in the past few years."

"Like what?"

He pulled the sheet more securely across his lap. "Like basing relationships on more than attraction and assumptions that the two of you have similar goals. Like knowing the difference between lust and compatibility."

"And you think we have compatibility?"

"Yes, but we also have lust. The difference is that we're adults and we can handle it. Neither one of us wants to jeopardize their career over a scandal."

"What happened at your house wasn't a scandal," she defended, raising her chin a notch. "I could have ignored the talk."

"I could have also, but we both agreed an engagement would be best."

"And you haven't had any second thoughts?" she asked.

"No." Surprisingly, he hadn't. Being committed to Amy seemed right, especially since they could talk so openly about their individual goals and needs. "Have you?"

She looked away, worry crinkling her forehead. "I don't know if they're really second thoughts, but yes, I've thought about our situation a lot."

"I've thought about it, too, but in the best way." He reached for her hand. "You make me feel good, Amy."

She turned her head to him, her eyes softening. "That's very sweet. Are you so sure you want to take such a huge step?"

"Yes."

"We're talking about real commitment here. Not some temporary living situation until you find someone else more glamorous, more exciting."

"I don't need more excitement or glamour. You provide plenty of both."

She frowned at him. "I'm not going into marriage believing divorce is the easy way out."

"Certainly not."

"I want children."

"Let's wait a year or so to get settled." The idea of children terrified him at the moment, but he was sure he'd grow into the concept of small versions of himself and Amy. He wasn't sure he'd be a good father, since his role models hadn't been steady, loving or compatible for the small-town life he now enjoyed. The idea of getting Amy pregnant, however, had definite appeal. He was sure she'd be a great mother, even with the demands of her medical practice. Sure, they could talk about children later.

"Why are you being so agreeable?"

"Because we *are* in agreement. Why don't you believe how much we have in common?"

"I don't know." She put her hand to her temple. "I just don't know, Gray. Marriage is so... permanent."

"As it should be." He paused, then took her hand. "Are you afraid you'll find someone else? Someone who would make your heart beat faster?"

"No," she said vehemently. "That's not my fear."

"Then what is?"

AMY TOOK A DEEP BREATH before answering, feeling both elated and frightened by what Gray had asked. Marriage. She hadn't expected him to want to make their relationship permanent. She wasn't ready for this, but she needed to explain.

"First, in order for you to understand where I am right now, I have to tell you about the past."

He squeezed her hand. "Okay."

His kindness and compassion, on top of his crazy, unexpected proposal, almost made her cry. Closing her eyes to blank out the sight of him naked, cross-legged on the bed, with only the corner of a sheet keeping him decent, was more than her overcharged emotions could take.

"When my mother died, I had a hard time understanding why. I was a happy child; I'd never experienced loss or great sadness. My father was devastated, but together we pulled through. He had his position as the town's doctor, and the support of friends. I had him, only him. I became afraid that something might happen to him, too, and I'd be all alone. My mother was an orphan, and my father's parents were older when he was born, and had died several years earlier."

She took a deep breath. "I was the woman of the house after that. I worked very hard to keep everything calm and steady. I'd had enough turmoil in my young life. All I wanted was for things to stay the same.

"I'm still like that, Gray. The little girl inside of me doesn't want her life to change. I'd barely gotten settled in Ranger Springs, and then I had to start a pretend dating relationship with you."

At his frown, she shook her head. "I didn't mean it that way. The pretend dating was my idea, after all. It seemed the smart thing for both of us, but it did upset my life."

"Played havoc with mine a time or two," Gray said with a wry smile.

"I know." She looked down as their clasped hands. "What I'm trying to say is that I took a chance on changing our relationship from pretend dating to lovers, and look what happened. First, we had to get engaged, then—"

"We didn't *have* to get engaged. I talked you into it, and you agreed because it's what you wanted."

"That's one way of looking at it."

"I know that's the truth, whether you want to admit it or not. You want to get married."

She briefly considered denying it, but knew she couldn't without lying. She *had* thought about marrying Gray. She'd admitted to herself that she didn't want the temporary engagement to end. "Maybe, but it means more change. I've had so much in my life recently. I'm not sure I'm ready for more."

Gray grasped both of her hands, forcing her to look at him. "Just answer this—does it feel right?"

"I don't know. I can't trust my feelings."

"Why?"

She shifted on the bed, wanting to pull away, but knowing she had to answer. She had to make him understand. "Because if I need you, you might leave me. I can't trust those feelings to last. I can't risk falling in love, only to lose you."

"I'm not going anywhere," he said, tipping her chin up so she had to look at him. "And I'm not expecting you to love me right now. I think we have something that's more important than a fleeting emotion. We have compatibility, friendship and passion. I think we're much better equipped to begin a marriage than a couple who simply claim to be in love."

What he said made sense, in a bizarre sort of way. She'd never thought of marriage in that manner. Her parents, she knew, had loved each other. That's why her mother's death had been so devastating.

"Believe me, what we have will last longer than some youthful ideal of love everlasting."

Gray had never mentioned love, even as an endearment, even in a moment of passion. *Surely he'd loved his first wife.* Was the experience so bad that he didn't want to repeat it? Amy knew one thing; he didn't love *her*. She couldn't let him know how deeply she felt about him. She'd learned to guard her heart.

After her mother had died, she'd carefully shown her father how much she cared for him without burdening him with emotional needs he would have struggled to fulfill. He had his own feelings of loss to contend with. Being considerate meant not demanding constant reassurances that she was loved. She knew her father loved her without him constantly telling her so.

She wasn't sure how Gray felt about her, but she knew he cared. He showed her in so many ways. So what if they didn't call it love?

"Maybe you're right about youthful ideals not lasting, but can you be so sure that you'll never fall in love with someone else?"

"Amy, I'll never be unfaithful to you. It's not in

my nature. If you'll agree to be my wife, I'll never put myself in the situation to look at someone else." He lay his palm along her cheek. "And I expect the same of you."

"Of course." She had no intention of being unfaithful to her husband, whoever he might be. And she knew his answer didn't really address the issue. If he didn't believe in love, how could he believe he'd fall for someone else?

"Then you'll say yes?"

"Gray...I just don't know."

"Trust your instincts, Amy."

"I'm a person who believes in science, in medicine. I don't treat my patients through sorcery, and I don't make decisions in my life based on feelings."

"Then apply logic to our relationship. All the reasons for getting married are obvious. Aren't the reasons *not* to take this engagement to its logical conclusion emotional?"

She couldn't argue with his logic. Besides, she wanted to marry him. She wanted the freedom to lie in his arms at night, wake beside him in the morning. She wanted to say to the world that he was her husband, to wear his ring and know that he was faithful only to her.

She wanted to make love to him, spend the night with him, wake up beside him each morning.

She wanted to give her father grandchildren.

"All right," she whispered. "I'll marry you."

He framed her face with his hands, looking deeply into her eyes. His own were dark and intense. Then he closed the gap between them, his lips taking hers in a fierce kiss. She closed her eyes, allowing herself to be swept away. He pressed her back against the pillows, the sheet falling away with her doubts, her lingering inhibitions.

She was going to be Mrs. Grayson Phillips. Dr. Amy Wheatley Phillips. She would keep the clinic and create a wonderful, calm life for herself and the family they'd have someday.

Life was going to settle down soon, she thought as his lips moved to her neck. She was going to be Gray's wife.

A WEEK LATER, LIFE WAS anything but calm. Robin and Ethan Parker insisted on hosting an engagement party in Amy and Gray's honor, but Joyce also wanted to be involved. They divided up duties into food, beverages, decorations and invitations, but needed frequent consultations with the bride-to-be. Fortunately, the weather stayed clear, cool and sunny, and everyone scurried about with their planning, as happy as could be.

Amy had her usual load of patients to see—all of whom, even Mrs. Gresham, added their hearty congratulations—plus she had to contend with her father's occasional visits to her office. He would stand in the doorway and grin as though *he* were the one getting married.

Well, maybe he should. Planning a wedding would certainly take his mind off her engagement, and his constant questions about when she and Gray were going to set the date. Where they were going to live. When they were going to have children.

She needed Gray's input about the most important detail—when the wedding should take place.

"I don't care," he said when she asked him at dinner the next weekend. "Would you like to be a June bride?"

"Isn't that awfully soon?"

"Is it?"

She knew what he was asking: Is there a reason you don't want to get married? She didn't know how to answer the unspoken question. Yes, she wanted to marry him, but she didn't want to rush into another change. Not until she was absolutely certain that Gray was committed to their union. His desire to get married just seemed so...impulsive. He wasn't the type of person who made rash decisions, much less took impetuous action. This whole marriage idea seemed so sudden, so unexpected.

But still, she found herself saying, "June would be fine."

And so the arrangements began. A small engagement party for friends and family was scheduled at Ethan and Robin's house. Life returned to a semblance of normalcy except some additional shopping trips to San Antonio and Austin on the weekends. She had to choose a dress, flowers, and decide who would stand up in the ceremony with her.

Gray had already asked Ethan to be his best man. Amy wasn't sure whom she would ask to be her maid of honor since so many of her high school friends had moved away from Ranger Springs. Her college roommate was a possibility, but they weren't as close as they once were due to demands of their respective careers. Her lack of close friends at this stage in her life was probably a sad commentary on how much she'd invested in becoming a doctor.

"You'll have a chance to make new friends," Gray told her when she mentioned her observation to him one evening. "We'll probably socialize more with Ethan and Robin since we'll be a real couple. And I have other business associates and casual friends who are married. Maybe after we're married you'll enjoy their company."

A real couple. She hadn't thought of that. She'd been concentrating on herself and Gray as individuals, but rarely on what they would mean together. They'd be looked at differently by friends, relatives, and acquaintances. People would start saying "Gray and Amy" as easily as they now said "Ethan and Robin."

He turned to her and grinned. "Are you ready to meet your future in-laws?"

Another detail of her new life she'd forgotten.

"We really need to tell them before they find out from someone else," he added.

"Shouldn't we invite them to the party?"

"Not unless you want to give my mother a heart attack. We need to break the news very calmly, in person."

Amy sighed. "I'm looking forward to meeting them, really I am, but I hadn't thought about having in-laws."

"My mother will want to take you shopping at her favorite designer stores. My stepfather will insist you meet with his financial advisor to set up a 401K plan for the clinic. My father...well, we'll have to catch him when he's between wives or trips abroad."

"Sounds...interesting."

"I'm no doctor, but I'd suggest we take my family in small doses."

Amy laughed. "I'll remember that. Should we plan a weekend trip to Dallas soon?"

"I need to go up there on business in about two weeks. Why don't you go with me then and we'll break the news. We'll spend one night at my mother's house, and see if my father is back in town and available for lunch the next day."

Gray didn't seem concerned about his family's reaction to the news he was getting married again. She thought they should tell his parents immediately, but apparently Gray had his reasons. Since everyone in Ranger Springs was elated, Amy wasn't worried about anyone on her side of the aisle throwing a fit. All in all, the planning was going pretty well. By the second week in January, she even got into a rhythm of shopping, consulting with Gray and decision making.

Amy reserved Bretford House for the ceremony and wedding dinner afterward. They'd decided on an early evening ceremony since June could be brutally hot and they wanted to have the service outside, just like Ethan and Robin's wedding. Between patient appointments and paperwork, she looked over menus and flowers, paper stock and engraving styles. The wedding plans became a part of her life, and she started believing it was really going to happen.

She was going to be Gray's wife.

THE ENGAGEMENT PARTY was a huge success, with mutual friends and neighbors from Ranger Springs and surrounding countryside attending. In a rare show of spite, Amy had an invitation sent to Mary-anne Bridges and her husband. To her surprise, the couple showed up.

"No, I'm really not interested in selling the clinic," Amy explained for the second time.

Her father walked up. "Dr. Bridges," he greeted the man who was only about ten years younger than him. "Maryanne," he smiled. "Why, I remember when you used to be a cheerleader in Wimberley."

Maryanne smiled, but she looked uncomfortable. "That was years ago."

"Seems like yesterday to me." Amy thought her father was overdoing the country doctor routine a bit, but she wasn't about to say anything.

"Daddy, Maryanne and her husband are buying up clinics in the area. I told them we weren't interested in selling."

"Damn right! Why, that's the dumbest thing I've ever heard. Excuse me. I've got to talk to Joyce." He stalked off, shaking his head.

Gray walked up at that moment, smiling in that devastating way of his, looking far too handsome in a lightweight cashmere sweater and black wool slacks. When she'd touched his shoulders earlier, the fabric had felt so soft she'd wanted to run her hands over every inch of him. Maybe later he'd let her explore the difference between the delicate knit and the hard muscled body beneath.

Maryanne seemed to have noticed too. An audible sigh escaped her before she schooled the dreamy look in her eyes. *So, she's jealous.* Amy felt a bit spiteful when she looped her arm through Gray's, showing her engagement ring, and smiled up at him.

"Having fun?" she asked.

"Now that I'm with you," he replied easily, bestowing such a hot look that she thought her wine might begin to boil in the glass. Leave it to Gray to come up with the perfect response—especially in front of her old nemesis.

Amy had done a lot of thinking about her past since she'd come home to Ranger Springs. One of her realizations involved Maryanne. She'd never understood until recently why she'd felt so competitive about the other girl. Since they didn't live in the same town, they hadn't met until they were in their teens, after Amy's mother had died. Maryanne had seemed to have it all—two loving parents, the most fashionable clothes, scholastic and sport successes and all the best friends. Amy had been dealing with more mature issues, like taking care of her father. Maryanne had acted as though she was friendly, but Amy soon realized she liked to compare and contrast herself to others, especially around mutual friends. *Especially around boys.*

She and Gray took their leave from the Bridges, circulating around the party. They talked to Pastor Carl about conducting the ceremony, to Ralph about setting up a joint account at the bank and Thelma about putting the proper notices in the paper. Everyone from Gina Summers, who asked if they were interested in getting a new house, to Jimmy Mack Branson, who suggested an economical honeymoon in nearby Aquarena Springs, congratulated them.

The town was firmly behind this union, and Amy began to relax and believe that any lingering doubts were groundless, and the future was going to be great.

THE POST-NEW YEAR RESPITE from winter came to an end when a windy cold front moved in from the northwest, combining with some gulf moisture. Meteorologists from both San Antonio and Austin predicted bad weather, so Amy and Gladys made sure the clinic was well stocked. More sprains and breaks could always be expected when rare icy precipitation hit the Hill Country. If it snowed, there was even a possibility of a heart attack from someone not accustomed to shoveling his or her steps or walk.

Heavy clouds moved in and icy winds whipped through the bare-branched trees. Amy was just about to leave the clinic for the night, bundled into a downy jacket and scarf, when the phone rang. She almost let the answering machine pick it up, but because she didn't have plans until later since Gray was gone to a business meeting in Austin, she put her purse down and picked up the phone.

"Wheatley Medical Clinic. Dr. Amy Wheatley speaking."

"Dr. Wheatley, this is Austin Memorial Hospital. There's been an accident..."

Chapter Thirteen

Ethan hadn't come to a complete stop before Amy threw off her seat belt and bolted from the car. He'd driven her in his Bronco to Austin. The hospital's emergency entrance was illuminated in bright red letters covered in a thin sheet of ice. Only the salt pellets that maintenance had sprinkled on the walkway earlier prevented her from sprawling face-first on the concrete as she ran toward the glass doors.

"Dr. Amy Wheatley," she said breathlessly to the triage nurse. "You have a patient here, Grayson Phillips. I was called."

"Yes, he's in X-ray right now. Down the hall to—"

Amy was already running down the beige tile, looking at the signs. She'd never practiced out of this hospital, so she wasn't familiar with the floor plan. But they were all similar, these emergency rooms and related services. She'd find Gray.

"Amy, wait!"

She heard Ethan's voice behind her, and then his footsteps pounding up the hallway, but she didn't stop. He'd catch up to her soon. She had to find Gray. She had to see his condition for herself.

Fortunately Ethan was still wearing his uniform, so no one would question him. In fact, if anyone gave her any trouble, it was reassuring to know she had an armed law enforcement officer beside her.

The last time she'd been in a hospital emergency room as a visitor, not a physician, she'd been a young girl. She'd walked in with Pastor Carl Schlepinger, who'd driven her to the hospital because her daddy was already here. Was already at the bedside of his wife, who'd never gained consciousness after her car accident.

She'd gotten there just after her mother was pronounced dead. Her father had been in shock. She'd never seen him like that, so devastated, so lost.

She imagined she looked very similar at this moment.

"Grayson Phillips," she asked breathlessly to the person at the X-ray desk. "Car accident."

The young woman looked slowly through forms attached to clipboards across the desk.

Amy rushed into the hallway leading to the exam rooms.

"You can't go back there."

"I'm a doctor," Amy called back to her.

"Wait!"

"Let her go," Ethan commanded. "She needs to be near him."

Although they'd barely spoken on the ride to Austin in his four-wheel-drive vehicle, she knew he was worried about his friend.

"Grayson Phillips?" she asked a technician. The

young woman pointed to the second exam room. The red light wasn't on, so Amy slipped inside.

''Gray?'' she whispered.

''We don't allow visitors back here!''

Amy peered across the room divider. All she could see from this angle was a draped body on a gurney. ''I'm a doctor...and his fiancée. Is he conscious?''

''Yes. Now please, stay back. I need to do another film.''

''Amy?'' The weak voice sounded so different than Gray's usual well-modulated, commanding baritone that she wanted to weep.

''I'm here. Just stay still.'' Her voice broke. ''I'll be outside when you're finished.''

She forced herself to turn away, push open the door and stumble into the hallway. Tears stung her eyes as she walked along, staring at the beige speckled tile. She sensed a presence, looked up and found Ethan standing at the intersecting halls.

''How is he?''

''I don't know. He's conscious, but he sounds so weak. They were doing a C spine—a skull and cervical spine x-ray—but I couldn't talk to him because the tech was working on him.''

''How long will he be inside X-ray?''

''I don't know. Maybe just one more film.'' She took a deep breath, wiping her eyes. ''I need to find his doctor.''

''Let's wait for him here. Then we can walk back to the ER with him.''

Amy nodded. *Please, let Gray be safe.* She felt so helpless, torn between her desire to find medical information and her need to stay by the man she loved.

Oh God, she did love him. She'd fallen in love with Gray despite all her warnings to guard her heart. What would he say if she told him how she felt? Should she tell him? No, she couldn't put him in the situation where he'd be faced with her feelings. He needed time to figure out how he felt. Time to grow to love her too, without pressure.

First, he needed time to heal.

A few minutes later, the door opened and Gray was wheeled out into the hallway. Amy couldn't stop herself from running to his side, from laying her palm along his cheek. The other side of his face was bruised, with butterfly closures from his cheekbone to his hairline.

She tried to smile, but failed miserably. "Oh, Gray."

"I'll bet I'm a sight."

"Don't worry," she said, trying to hold back her tears as she walked next to the gurney, "you'll look worse tomorrow."

"Gee, thanks, Doc," he said as cheerfully as possible, considering his obviously painful contusions. "I didn't know you had such a great bedside manner."

She sniffled. "I do my best to be informative." She turned to the tech, who continued to push Gray down the hall, back toward the ER. "Who is his attending?"

"Dr. Rashid."

"I'm going to stay with you. Ethan's here, too. He's right ahead," she explained, because Gray couldn't turn his head. "He brought me in his four-wheel-drive because I didn't want to end up in here with you."

"The roads are terrible."

She smiled, sniffling again. "You should have stayed in Austin."

"I wanted to come home to you."

"Watch out," the tech said as they reached the double doors into the ER. Amy stayed back, wiping her eyes, crying silently. Ethan came up and put his arm around her.

"He's going to be okay."

"He wanted to come home to me," Amy whispered.

"Of course he did." He handed her a clean folded handkerchief. "Come on. Let's go talk to his doctor."

GRAY WAS ADMITTED TO the hospital overnight for observation due to a concussion, two bruised ribs, a laceration on his face and a dislocated kneecap. All in all, he felt pretty lucky. The Lexus was still at the bottom of the ravine and probably would be until the roads cleared and it could be towed to the dealership. Thank God he'd been able to call for help on his cell phone. They'd had a terrible time getting him out of the car and up the steep embankment, and he'd felt each jarring motion, each pull and tug on his bruised body.

With all the pain medication he'd now been given, he barely felt his various injuries. And Amy was beside him.

"I'm sorry I put you through this. You were

right—I should have stayed in Austin when I realized the roads were getting worse."

"This wasn't your fault. You're one of the safest drivers I know."

"Thank you."

"You're welcome," she answered, stroking his hand where a stained patch of skin had once held an IV.

"I mean for everything. For coming so quickly, even though the roads must have been worse for you and Ethan than they were when I had the wreck. And for talking to my doctors, checking up on my injuries."

"It was the least I could do. Besides, that's what I'm trained for. Believe me, it's easier to react as a medical professional in a situation like this than when someone you...care for is hurt."

He turned his hand so he was holding hers. "Your mother died in a car accident, didn't she? This must have brought back terrible memories."

Amy nodded. "You'd think the hospital was the last place I'd want to spend any time, but I suppose I reacted just the opposite of some people. I knew the doctors had done everything they could. My father explained her injuries so I wouldn't wonder how she died. He thought it was better that I understand she wasn't in any pain at the end."

She stroked his temple near the butterfly closures. "Like you, she had a head injury, but hers was massive. There were no airbags then, and she hated wearing her seat belt. She always complained that it was uncomfortable and wrinkled her clothes."

Gray nodded. He'd heard similar complaints from

others, but he'd always worn his seat belt. It was the law in Texas, but it also made sense.

"She bled out from internal injuries before paramedics could get her stabilized. At least she was unconscious. She didn't know what was happening to her."

"Your father must have been devastated."

"He was. The experience was so terrible, but it made us closer."

"And now you want to please him."

She shrugged. "I suppose I've always wanted to please my dad, but I don't think that's so bad. He'd a good father. He had a rough time right after my mother died, but he bounced back and we did okay, just the two of us."

"Are you sure you aren't marrying me to please him?" Gray wasn't sure if the medication had loosened his lips, or if the accident had just cast a new light on the situation, but he needed to know.

"I've thought about it. Until today, I wasn't really sure."

"You mean the accident?" He frowned. "I don't understand."

She took a deep breath, looking away from their clasped hands to stare into the darkness outside the window. "When I got the phone call, I was so worried. I have to admit that I thought of my mother, and how it felt to rush to the emergency room, only to discover half of your life was gone. But when I saw you lying in X-ray, so weak and pale, so unlike I'd ever seen you before, I realized…"

"Go on," he said.

She turned back to him, her blue eyes shiny with unshed tears. "I realized I love you."

He wasn't ready to hear this. He clasped her hand tighter, but he couldn't look into her eyes any longer. He couldn't bear to see what had been right in front of him for days, maybe weeks: Amy believed she was in love with him.

He couldn't tell her the words she wanted to hear, not without lying. He cared about her, certainly. He enjoyed being with her in every sense. But love? That was a myth, something created to make people believe in fairy-tale endings or keep them committed to each other through guilt.

He wasn't going to lie to her. He couldn't say he'd suddenly changed his mind; now he believed in romantic love.

"It's okay," she whispered. "I don't expect you to tell me anything. I know how you feel."

He looked into her weary, resigned eyes and wondered how she could know something that had eluded him for years: his true feelings.

SHE SHOULDN'T HAVE TOLD him, Amy realized as soon as the words left her mouth. Confessing her love was not the way to make her life calm and secure. Just when wedding activities had subsided to a manageable level, when everyone in town had stopped declaring their amazement that she and Gray were getting married, she'd thrown a monkey wrench into the works.

Now Gray looked at her differently. Oh, he'd never admit it, but she could see his reservations in his stormy eyes. When she'd visited the hospital first thing the next morning, he was polite, warm, but not the Gray she'd known since November. He'd even suggested she go on back to the clinic because he'd asked Ethan to drive him back home when he was released.

She'd tried to keep the hurt out of her voice and hide her expression from his eyes, but she didn't know if she'd been successful. He was trying even harder to maintain control and she didn't know what to do.

Ethan had called her around four o'clock to report Gray was home and looking forward to seeing her later. As soon as the clinic closed for the day, she drove to the Four Square Café, picked up a container of their chicken vegetable soup and a couple of pieces of pecan pie, and headed for Gray's house.

The ice that had blanketed the area yesterday was gone, so the curving road up the hill wasn't difficult to negotiate. She parked in the circular drive and debated whether to ring the doorbell. If he was resting, she didn't want to disturb him. Walking on his injured knee would be difficult.

She tried the front door; it was unlocked. Easing inside, she looked around. Gray was asleep on the couch, an Indian print blanket covering him. On the coffee table sat a bottle of water and two bottles of prescription medicine. Apparently Ethan had gotten everything set up nicely before he left.

Amy tiptoed past the living room and entered the kitchen. She'd never needed to locate anything in this room, but Gray's utensils, pots and pans were as orderly as everything else in his life. She had no trouble heating up the soup and making hot tea. In the cupboard she found crackers, salt and pepper.

"Ethan?"

"No, it's Amy," she answered. She walked back into the living room to find Gray propping himself up against the back of the couch. He looked uncomfortable, to say the least. She imagined he was in pain, despite the medication. "How are you feeling?"

"Like I rolled my car down a hill," he answered, attempting a smile. "Thank goodness for air bags."

"Have you taken anything?"

Gray nodded, then winced at the movement. "Before Ethan left."

He wasn't even looking at her. This man, who had always given her undivided attention, now found it difficult to meet her eyes. Oh, she knew she was being silly. He was in pain, he felt helpless, and his life had been disrupted. Still, she felt disappointed. In her own way, she was as helpless as Gray to change the situation.

"I brought some dinner. Something light, something a bit more decadent," she said cheerfully.

"Sounds good. They didn't bring me much in the hospital."

"I'll get you a tray."

"I can get up." He pushed up from the cushions.

She placed a hand on his arm. "There's no need. You should rest your knee and your ribs."

He slumped back, looking up at her for the first time. "You're the doctor."

She turned away so he didn't see the disappointment on her face. Now she was a doctor, not his fiancée, not his lover. It's just the accident, she tried to tell herself. This was temporary. After he felt better, things would return to normal.

But as she finished heating the soup, she wondered if anything would be the same, or if Gray would forever resent her declaration of love.

Chapter Fourteen

"No, Mother, I'm fine. Just a little sore and bruised."

"Maybe you should come back to Dallas and have our specialists look at you, Gray. You can't possibly be receiving the best medical care in that small town."

He looked across the room at Amy, who was adding another log to the fire. She'd given him excellent medical care, plus provided for every personal need. She'd been perfect.

"Believe me, Mother, the medical care here is excellent."

Amy turned, gave him a shy smile, and walked across to sit on the other end of the couch.

"I'll call you in a week or so and we'll make new plans. Good night, Mother."

After she said good night and he hung up the phone, he turned to Amy. "She's taking the news pretty well. I suppose I'm lucky she didn't see me," he said, touching the bruise on his cheekbone. As Amy had predicted, his bruises and abrasions now looked even worse than immediately after the accident.

"You didn't mention the engagement," Amy said, her tone more tentative than usual.

"I'd rather tell them in person. I've learned over the years not to break important news to them over the phone."

"So a potentially fatal car accident isn't serious, but an engagement is?"

She sounded a bit angry, not at all like Amy.

"That's not what I meant. The call was to cancel a weekend visit, not to tell them any specifics," he answered calmly.

Amy shook her head. "I suppose I don't understand your relationship with your parents."

"There's really nothing to understand. We get along very well as long as we're not forced into intimate situations."

"I see." She stood up, adjusting her sweater and chinos. "Well, if you don't need me for anything else, I'll be going."

"What's your rush?"

"I have an early day tomorrow."

He couldn't stop a frown, but decided not to push the issue. Amy had done so much for him that any quibbling would be petty. She was probably tired. Maybe he should have asked her to stay the night these past two days, but with his injuries, he'd spent most of the time on the couch, his knee propped up on pillows. She'd come for lunch, and then back at night both days.

"Thank you again for everything. When I get better, I'm going to make this up to you."

Amy grew very still, standing beside the couch with wounded eyes. "This isn't a competition. No one's keeping score."

"That's not what I—"

"I have to go," she said, twirling away from him.

"Amy, don't go!"

"I have to. I'll call you tomorrow."

SHE BARELY MADE IT OUT the door before the tears began. She knew he was hurting and on meds that could alter anyone's disposition. As a doctor she should excuse his comments to her and his mother. But as a woman—his fiancée—she sensed a change unrelated to his accident or his injuries. Something was wrong, terribly wrong, with their relationship. She shouldn't have told him how she felt. Her confession of love was now a wedge between them. He couldn't forget what she'd said, and she wouldn't take the words back. How could she, when they were true?

Wrenching open the door to her car, she sat very still for a moment while she tried to calm down enough to drive. She had to get out of here soon, before Gray noticed the car hadn't left the drive and tried to hobble out. He didn't need the strain on his knee, plus she didn't think she could face his questions about why she'd run out.

We get along very well as long as we're not forced into intimate situations. How very telling. He'd been brought up to be distant, reserved. He'd created such a powerful persona that everyone wanted to go out with him, and once they did, they wanted the challenge of getting the second date. The one he'd never granted until she came along and offered their pretend dates.

No one's keeping score. Wrong. Everyone had been keeping score all along. The town, her dad, and even herself. She'd scored the biggest prize, Prince Charming, the man everyone else wanted. The funny thing was, she didn't want him if it meant she could never expect him to open up, to share himself as she wanted to share herself.

Inserting the key, she started the engine and revved it a few times to let him know she was leaving. When her hands were steady, when her vision was no longer distorted by tears, she put the car into gear and drove away from Gray's house.

Confronting Gray when he was still recovering would be unfair. She'd wait until he was better, then talk to him about how he felt. She wondered if he could overlook the fact his fiancée was in love with him, or if that would, ironically, become an irreparable wedge between them.

WHEN AMY CAME BACK THE next day, Gray knew she was trying to be as normal and casual as possible. She inspected his injuries, commented on his improved mobility and encouraged him to keep up the good work.

She acted just like any other competent, caring physician. Where was his sweet fiancée, the woman who believed she was in love with him?

He'd done something to disappoint her, but damned if he knew what. They'd been talking about his slightly dysfunctional family, then about not mentioning the engagement. His reasons were perfectly logical, and if she knew his mother, Amy would understand. There was no way he could casually mention he'd asked someone to marry him.

He couldn't remember anything he'd said that would have made Amy so unhappy. When he'd tried to talk about what was wrong, she'd claimed nothing. She'd said it innocently, as clear-eyed as possible for someone who wasn't a good liar.

Dammit, he didn't know how to make her talk to him.

When she came back that night, he was off the pain pills. His knee no longer throbbed, his head wasn't hurting, and he was determined to communicate with Amy—perhaps in the way that worked best.

AMY SENSED A DIFFERENCE in Gray as soon as she walked in the door. His gaze followed her as she put together dinner. He spoke politely as they ate, asking about her day, but his eyes held a hunger for something beyond chicken pot pies and peach cobbler.

She tried her best to be cheerful, but she had a suspicion he knew something was wrong. Had he figured out why she'd rushed out of his house two days ago? If so, would he say anything? They'd never had this type of tension between them, even during that first date.

"I'll help you," he said as she began to clear the dishes.

"Your knee."

"It feels much better. I need to be up and around on it a little."

"Well, be careful."

In no time they had the dishes in the dishwasher, the remaining cobbler in the commercial-grade refrigerator and the towel neatly folded across the pristine, seamless counters in his high-tech kitchen. She flipped off the light, ready to go into the living room, when Gray came up behind her.

"I've missed you," he murmured against her neck, just below her ear.

Shivers ran across her skin as his arms encircled her waist. "Gray! What are you doing?"

"Am I that much out of practice?"

"But...your injuries."

"My doctor, who is very talented, by the way, claims I'm almost as good as new."

"I don't remember saying that."

"Close enough," he said before trailing his lips down her neck. She'd worn a loose cowl-neck sweater, which he had no trouble pushing aside to continue his quest downward.

She tried to muster up some anger. After all, they couldn't solve problems with sex. But his hands had moved up to her breasts, cupping her, and his lips continued to torment that sensitive spot where her shoulder and neck joined, and they'd been apart for so long.

And, after all, she loved him.

"I'm not up to carrying you up the stairs tonight, but would you consider joining me on the couch?"

"It depends," she said, closing her eyes against the exquisite sensations of him teasing her nipples into tight buds, "on what you have in mind."

"My intentions are purely dishonorable."

"In that case, yes." She grabbed his hands and

reluctantly pulled them to her waist. Smiling back over her shoulder, she walked toward the couch where he'd spent so many hours recently. Tonight, she'd give him some happy memories of those cushions. And maybe, in the aftermath, when their hearts were beating as one, they would regain the feeling of closeness they'd lost in the past few days.

Maybe he'd realize there was more to their relationship than keeping the town happy, enjoying the Hill Country and sharing some pretty spectacular passion.

THE NEXT DAY GRAY returned to his office for a few hours, catching a ride until his knee was dependable enough to drive. And until he got a replacement car while his insurance company settled the claim.

His staff had kept the business running fine with only a few daily phone calls and e-mails from him, but getting back to work felt good. As he'd told Amy, he loved this company like it was his family. He'd actively developed the technology, he'd hired the best managers and he'd worked hard to create a climate of trust and cooperation among the high-tech workers.

While he waited for his marketing manager to finish up for the afternoon and pull his car around to the front, Gray had time to think. As well as things were going at the office, he couldn't say the same for his personal life. Last night he and Amy had made sweet, slow love on his couch. He'd encouraged her to be bold, and she hadn't hesitated to take the lead. He got a funny feeling in his chest when he remembered how she'd looked, lying naked above him, taking him into her body. How her eyes had drifted close, how her sigh had mingled with his.

He got aroused just remembering the night. But as much as he'd enjoyed making love, he felt as though she were waiting for something else. The tension that had been in the air earlier returned, slowly but surely, as their overheated bodies cooled and their heart rates returned to normal.

She wanted to say "the words" again, but wouldn't. He could tell. He knew Amy better than he had ever imagined he'd know another person. She had the most honest, expressive face. Once she'd told him she was a terrible liar, and he believed her. He wondered how she'd ever deceived her father about their relationship.

He propped his knee up on another chair he'd pulled close and looked out the windows of his corner office. The hills stretched out in a rolling sea of tan and beige, with occasional outcropping of gray rocks and faded green live oaks. Spring couldn't come fast enough for him. He wanted to see everything burst to life, to shake off the drab colors of winter and become a showplace once more.

He wanted to see summer come to the Hill Country, and with it, his wedding. He waited for the sense of panic he always anticipated when thinking of marriage, but it didn't materialize. He did feel a sense of unease, however, when he thought about Amy. She had high expectations for this union. With every decision she made about dresses or announcements or flowers, she got one step closer to the romanticized version of happily-ever-after. If she wanted him to go into the occasion with the same romantic notions, she would be disappointed. As far as he was concerned, they were getting married for very logical, sound reasons. No amount of flowers or ribbons would change the fact that he and Amy were two very compatible people. He certainly hoped she could understand and accept his feelings on this issue.

"Mr. Phillips," his administrative assistant called from the doorway, "your ride is here."

He pushed aside thoughts of Amy and the wedding for now. His half day at the office had left him tired and out of sorts, and he needed to get home, take a pain pill and stop thinking about the brief flash of disappointment he'd seen in Amy's eyes last night.

ON FRIDAY EVENING, Amy and Gray accepted an invitation to dinner at Robin and Ethan's house. Since Gray was feeling much better and his bruises were fading, she thought getting out was a good idea. He'd spent a few hours at the office on Friday, but she knew he was going stir-crazy in the house. He was a man used to an active life, so sitting around watching television or reading hardly kept him busy.

Besides, they needed a night out. The tension she'd felt upon entering his house Thursday evening hadn't dissipated after they'd made love. Having a friendly dinner in a casual setting was probably just what everyone needed.

She parked her car, watching Gray closely as he moved his legs to exit her much smaller vehicle. He didn't appear to be in pain from his knee, which was an excellent sign. He was healing fast. They could get on with the wedding plans and the announcement to his parents.

The thought caused her to draw in her breath at a funny, fluttering feeling in her stomach. First, she realized, they needed to eliminate this tension between them.

Gray rang the doorbell, then Ethan and Robin were both there, greeting them, making them welcome. The interior of the home was warm and spacious, decorated in a Southwest style Amy liked. The only thing out of place was a large recliner that she suspected had belonged to Ethan before the wedding, because it didn't look like anything a professional decorator like Robin would choose. Delicious smells drifted through the open floor plan of the house, making Amy's mouth water and her stomach grumble.

"We're having pot roast with vegetables," Robin said, tucking a strand of honey blond hair behind her ear. "I have to tell you now that Ethan is the cook in the family. He's been trying to teach me, but I'm still having trouble with anything harder than boiling water or microwaving popcorn."

Amy laughed at her admission. "I like to cook, but I'm hardly a gourmet chef. Gray, on the other hand, is highly suspect. The times he's cooked for me, the food was delicious. Far more tasty than one could expect from a bachelor."

"A confirmed bachelor at that," Ethan said, coming up behind his wife and putting his arms around her waist, splaying his fingers across her stomach. Robin turned her head and smiled at him, love shining from both their eyes.

Amy had to look away; the moment was so intense, so intimate.

"I'm divorced, remember?" Gray reminded his friend. He obviously hadn't noticed the loving exchange. Either that, or it didn't bother him in the least. "I'm supposed to be domesticated, unlike a true bachelor. You, on the other hand, are a freak of nature—a real bachelor who could cook, clean house and take care of the yard."

"Hey, my aunt and parents taught me well. That's one reason I was such a good catch for Robin. No wonder she chased me down so fast."

"Chased you down! I did no such thing!" She sounded more amused than outraged, Amy thought. Robin and Ethan truly had a wonderful relationship.

"Would you like a beer or some wine?" Ethan asked.

"Wine would be fine," Amy answered.

"For me too. I'm off those damned pain pills that made me goofy."

Maybe that had been the problem between them. Amy thought perhaps she'd imagined that her declaration had changed their relationship.

Ethan poured a red wine into two glasses, then grabbed a beer from the kitchen for himself. "You're not having anything?" Amy asked Robin as she passed out cocktail napkins.

"No, I..." She turned and looked at Ethan. "I suppose we should go ahead and tell them."

He came up and looped an arm around his wife's shoulders. "Go ahead, love."

"We're going to have a baby."

Amy knew she stood there for a few seconds, her

face blank and her voice mute. Then she forced a smile, genuinely pleased for the happy couple. "I'm so happy for you both," she finally said, taking Robin's hand. "Have you been to your ob-gyn?"

"Yes, last week. Everything's fine, so far."

"I'm sure it will be."

"Congratulations," Gray said, taking Robin's hand when Amy let go. "You'll be great parents."

"I hope so. It's a bit daunting."

"Ethan's the best candidate for dad of the year I've ever seen," Gray said, "and he's not even a father yet."

"Was that a backhanded compliment?" the lawman asked.

"Take it like you will," Gray said with a laugh.

"Hey, someday you'll be in this situation. I can't wait to make a few choice remarks about your qualifications."

A shadow passed over Gray's features, so fleeting that Amy wondered if anyone else noticed. No, probably not. Robin and Ethan were again gazing at each other with such love in their hearts that it was almost painful to watch.

And why should it be painful, Amy wondered? What an odd thought. She should be happy for them, excited about welcoming a new life into their family. But somehow, their happiness and Robin's pregnancy had somehow turned into a referendum on her, the dedicated small town doctor who was going to marry a man who didn't love her in return.

Forcing another smile, she placed her wineglass on the rustic buffet. "Would you excuse me a minute?"

"Down the hall to your right," Robin said instinctively.

Amy fled from the happy couple, from their wonderful news. She'd never realized until this very minute how much she needed to see Gray gaze at her with undisguised love in his eyes.

She shut the door of the guest bath and leaned against the wood. Could she settle for less? With a sick feeling in the pit of her stomach, she feared she knew the answer.

Chapter Fifteen

"What's wrong?" Gray asked again as Amy pulled her car to a stop in his driveway. "Please don't tell me 'nothing' again, because I know that's not true. Ever since you went into the bathroom at Robin and Ethan's house, you've been quiet and preoccupied."

She turned off the ignition, then turned to him in the darkness of the car's interior. "Seeing Robin and Ethan tonight made me think about us."

"In what way?"

"They seem so...happy."

"You aren't happy?" She'd seemed tense and nervous this week, but he'd chalked most of that up to his injury. Of course she'd thought about her mother's accident. And taking care of him every evening couldn't be much fun...except for Thursday night. They'd both enjoyed themselves. Or he'd thought they had.

"How can I answer?" She gripped the steering wheel as she nibbled on her bottom lip. "Ever since your accident, I've had to hold myself back. I can't tell you how I'm feeling, what I'm thinking."

"We've never had any problem talking to each

other. Why would we now?'' he asked, stroking her shoulder. Her muscles were as tight as a bodybuilder on steroids. ''Amy, what's wrong?''

She closed her eyes, took a deep breath, then looked at him. ''I love you, Gray. I know that wasn't part of our agreement, but it happened. It's hurting me to keep from saying it to you. I want to be free to tell you what's in my heart.''

He didn't want to discuss this now. Not in the car, not with her so upset. He felt trapped, as though a crushing weight pressed him all around him. He at least needed fresh air, but the night was too cold to open the windows, and besides, he needed to get out of the confines of the small car.

''Come inside. I'll make some coffee or tea, and we'll talk about it.''

''Let's talk about it now, here. If I come into the house, I'll lose my nerve. Or you'll kiss me and I'll forget what I need to say.''

''Amy, I don't know why we need to have this conversation now. If you need to say the words to me, go ahead. Do you think I'll be upset?''

''I have no idea! I've only seen you mildly upset once, and hardly over anything this major.''

''This isn't major.'' At her shocked expression, he continued. ''I mean, it's not major in a bad way. I respect your opinion of how you feel. If you need to say those words to me, I won't be upset.''

''Gray, I *love* you! Doesn't that mean anything to you?''

''I believe you *think* you're in love with me. I just don't happen to believe there is such a...thing as love.''

"What do you feel for me?" she asked, her tone determined and cautious at the same time.

"I feel many things for you," he answered carefully, the car suddenly smaller, more confining. "Respect, admiration, desire. How about those for starters?"

"But not love?"

The crushing feeling in the center of his chest intensified. "I don't believe in love. I think it's something we delude ourselves into believing so we can justify sex, or monogamy, or compatibility. What some people call love is just a set of circumstances that would produce the same result in any number of individuals with the same characteristics."

"You sound like a textbook from some parallel universe. How can you not believe that two people share something beyond common values and sexual attraction?"

"Because giving it a name makes it something almost sacred. Something that gives people excuses for doing things that are harmful."

"Love is powerful, but I don't think that's what you're describing."

"I just think it's a delusion, that's all! I thought I loved my wife, but I was just saying the words, going through the motions. I asked her to marry me because she was beautiful and I was attracted to her. I thought we wanted success and everything that went with it, but I was wrong."

"Yes, you were wrong, but mostly she was wrong for you. If the two of you really loved each other—"

"Right! Then she wouldn't have betrayed me with

my best friend. She wouldn't have told me that she was tired of competing with my business."

"She was angry and she did something wrong. That doesn't mean love is an illusion."

He shook his head. "Love is just some word that describes a weakness or a need, perhaps to control, sometimes to cause guilt."

"That's so cynical! You don't know anyone who's happily married? What about Ethan and Robin? What about your mother and stepfather?"

"Ethan and Robin are newlyweds. I hardly think they're a good example. And my mother? She and my stepfather have a mutually beneficial alliance. She's a great hostess and he provides plenty of money to maintain her lifestyle."

"What about my parents? They truly loved each other."

"I don't know about your parents, Amy. Maybe their commitment to each other was never tested."

She plunged her fingers into her hair, letting out an anguished moan. "I'm not delusional, Gray. I know what I'm feeling."

"Amy, I'm sorry. I just can't put a single name on a rather complex relationship."

"You mean you won't. You won't say the words so you don't have to risk your heart again. You won't believe because you're afraid to trust me."

"I trust you."

"Do you? What if I traveled extensively, or went to every medical conference that was offered? What if I spent time around other doctors—male doctors?"

He stiffened, the seat suddenly hard and uncomfortable. ''You have a strong sense of ethics. You wouldn't cheat on me.''

''Did you feel that same way about your wife before you discovered her betrayal?''

''That situation has nothing to do with us!''

''It has everything to do with us. I'm being cheated out of your love because of her infidelity!''

''You are nothing like my ex-wife!''

''But who am I? How do you feel about me?''

''You have my respect, my admiration and my trust. Isn't that enough?''

Her eyes glistened in the dim light. ''No.''

He looked at her a long time...or what seemed like a long time. His features seemed to turn to stone as he sat in her car, as he watched his hopes for the future evaporate in the cool night air.

She sniffed, breaking through the rigidity that kept him sitting there, watching, waiting for her to say she didn't mean they were finished because he couldn't say the words she wanted.

''We could have a good life, Amy,'' he said quietly. ''We have a lot going for us, but I'm not going to beg.''

''I need your love.''

''You're asking for too much.''

''No, I'm not.''

He reached for the door handle, all the while gazing into her expressive eyes. Those eyes that couldn't lie. She looked devastated, but she didn't cry. She simply watched him, her expression showing him that she was disappointed.

Disappointed? She was the one who was breaking

their engagement. She was the one who couldn't settle for everything he had to give.

"You could come in," he offered. He didn't want her to drive if she was so upset. Hell, he didn't want her to leave at all. Surely they could work this out.

"I'm fine. I'll be careful." She looked down at her hand, her eyes glistening. Before he knew what she was doing, she'd pulled off his engagement ring.

"No!"

"Take it. It's not mine to keep."

"It's yours," he said, wrenching open the door, nearly stumbling out of the car when his knee gave way. He didn't stop. He had to get away from her, before she could force him to take the ring, before she could end it forever.

With his lungs burning from that terrible pressure, he opened the door and walked inside his silent house.

AMBROSE WHEATLEY LIMPED into the Four Square Café, his spirits lower than a lovelorn toad. Just this Monday morning, he'd come into the clinic, feeling just fine, only to see Amy with red-rimmed eyes and a sorrowful expression. When she'd pushed her lanky hair off her face, he'd seen her ring finger as bare as a baby's bottom.

"What's wrong, Amy girl?" he'd asked.

"We broke up. He doesn't think he loves me."

"What! Of course that man loves you."

"I know, but he doesn't think so," she'd sobbed, and run into her office.

Gladys wasn't a bit of help. She'd shrugged her

shoulders and held up her hands, just as confused as he was.

He didn't know what to do except seek Joyce's advice. She was a woman. She'd understand what was going on. And if they couldn't put their heads together and come up with something, he was heading out to Gray's place. Nobody was stomping on his little girl's heart without answering to him.

Sure enough, Joyce and Thelma were sitting at their regular table, chatting up a storm.

"Ladies," he said, "we've got a problem." He explained what he knew to them and waited for an answer. Surely they'd know what to do. Hell, they were women!

"I don't understand, Ambrose," Thelma said. "It's clear to everyone that Amy and Gray are perfect for each other. Are you sure she didn't say anything before? Maybe about a fight or something he did to make her mad?"

"Not a thing. I was sure that things were goin' along just great."

"Ladies, Dr. Wheatley," Ethan Parker greeted them. The police chief was just about to walk by their table when Ambrose remembered he and Gray were good friends.

"Just a darn minute, Chief," Ambrose said. "We need to have a little talk about that low-down snake who broke my girl's heart."

AMY RETURNED HIS RING on Saturday via the nurse from the clinic. Gladys had handed it to him without a word and left. He'd stood there staring at the velvet box and wondering how something that had seemed so right could have gone so wrong.

He spent most of the weekend fuming about Amy's hardheaded attitude toward their relationship. How could she walk away from the best thing that had ever happened to either of them? Didn't she see that they were as perfect for each other as two people could be? Why did she have to insist on putting labels on what was basically a simple agreement? They'd get married, pursue their respective careers, have children when the time was right and build a good life for themselves in Ranger Springs. Simple. Why couldn't she see that?

When he went to bed Sunday night, his anger had faded. He wondered what she was doing, whether she was still upset. Were her eyes still filled with tears? Did she decide she was wrong after all—that she didn't love him?

Then he got mad at himself. Why would he be upset if she'd changed her mind? After all, she was deluding herself about love. Like most women, she'd needed some label to put on their relationship. Not that he thought she was planning on using it against him.

Amy wasn't petty or manipulative. She just wanted him to believe in a myth and then say the damn words. Every time he thought about laying himself open, he got that tight feeling again. He couldn't do it. He couldn't lie to her.

On Monday, Gray couldn't concentrate on the technical specifications his staff had written for electronic components of his new miniature receiver.

They could have been describing an aircraft carrier for all he knew.

"Dammit," he muttered. He eased his injured knee off the chair he was using as an ottoman and pushed away from the desk. His head ached, his knee hurt, and he wasn't getting anything done at the office. He might as well go home and sulk in private. Maybe he'd get it out of his system.

Maybe he'd get her out of his head.

"Fat chance," he muttered as he paused in front of his administrative assistant's office.

"What was that, Mr. Phillips?"

"I'm leaving for the day. Call me at home if there's an emergency."

He walked to the rental car that had been delivered this morning. It was beige and boring. He hated boring beige cars.

When he drove the obnoxious automobile in his garage, Ethan was waiting for him in the circular drive. He sincerely hoped no one was pressing legal charges because he'd run off the road. The only thing he'd destroyed—beside his Lexus—was a flimsy guardrail.

"What's going on?" he asked as he walked to where Ethan leaned against his black Bronco.

"I've been sent as an emissary for some concerned citizens in town."

"What kind of concerned citizens? I haven't done anything to worry anyone."

"Well, that's debatable," Ethan said, folding his arms across his chest. "There's word that your engagement to Amy is off."

"Dammit!" Gray turned away from his scowling friend and looked out across the rolling hills.

"Look, Amy and I had a discussion over what we each needed and wanted out of our relationship. It took me totally by surprise to learn that our goals weren't the same. Hell, all along, when we pre...well, when we were dating, I thought we had nearly everything in common."

"Let's go inside and talk about this. I know women can be perplexing. I didn't have a clue about what was going on in Robin's head until we both discovered how our aunts were matchmaking."

"Matchmakers!" Gray growled as he stalked toward the door. "I wish they'd never started interfering in our lives. Maybe Amy and I could have progressed in a more normal manner without the pressure."

Ethan followed him inside. "What are you talking about?"

Gray eased down on the sofa and propped his knee on the table. For the next few minutes, he explained the pretend dating, then the pretend engagement. He had a harder time when Ethan pressed for details on why he wanted to progress from a pretend, possibly long-term engagement to a rather quick wedding.

"I'll tell you what I told Amy—it just feels right."

"Are you the same Grayson Phillips who vowed never to get married again after what Connie did to you? I remember when you had to scrape together a settlement for her, about the same time you were expanding the business. You were up to your eyeballs in debt, but you didn't let her betrayal stop your dream."

"And Amy wouldn't interfere with my business either. One of the great things about our relationship is that we both have careers. Along with the ideals and goals we have in common, we could have had a great partnership."

"That all sounds fine and logical, but what about love? Isn't that why you ask someone to marry you."

Gray shifted on the coach. "Not necessarily."

"So you dated her for convenience, pretended to be engaged to her to save your reputations, then suddenly decide to get married because you have a few things in common and she won't mess with your business? Excuse me for being dense, but what's missing here?"

"Look, she thinks she's in love with me. It's a normal reaction, I suppose, after seeing me in the hospital after the accident. Her mother was killed in a car wreck, and I think Amy connected the two events in her mind. Hell, it was an emotional moment for her."

"But not for you."

Gray wanted to get up and pace, but his head was throbbing and his knee hurt from all the pointless wandering he'd done yesterday, while he'd been nursing his anger. "Look, you didn't know me back when I first met Connie in college, but we were inseparable. We had a lot going for us. Sex, for one thing. She supported my career choice and was excited when I decided to start my own company based on that first invention. I was under the delusion that I was a very happily married man."

"Until she decided to cheat on you with another man."

"And my best friend at the time, to boot. She'd fallen in love with him, she said, as though that explained everything."

"In her mind perhaps it did."

Gray ground his teeth and shot off the couch, ignoring his injuries. "Romantic love doesn't explain a damned thing. It's just an excuse to do what you wanted to do in the first place." He walked to the windows overlooking the hills. "I used love as a reason to marry her, when what I really meant was that I lusted after her and she didn't give me any grief. She used love as an excuse to forsake her marriage vows and betray me with my best friend. Hell, I trusted both of them!"

"You are one bitter man," Ethan said softly.

"I prefer to think of myself as enlightened. When Amy started talking about love, I didn't say anything negative. Only when she pushed me against the wall did I tell her how I felt."

"I'm sure that was the high point of her day."

"It wasn't my best moment either!"

"Hell, Gray, how can you say you don't love Amy? I've seen the way you two are together. I've seen the way you look at her sometimes when you're not putting on a show for the rest of the world."

"I don't know what you're talking about, and I don't think you do either."

"Can't you be open-minded about this? Amy knows how she feels."

"She knows how she's been conditioned to feel by a society obsessed with love. Do you know how many problems are caused by people who think they're doing the right thing in the name of love?"

"That has nothing to do with your situation, and I think you'd realize it if you'd quit trying so hard to convince yourself you aren't in love."

"I don't need to convince myself of anything. I admire, respect, trust and desire Amy. Why isn't that enough for her? Hell, why isn't it enough for you?"

"Because you're in denial. Amy knows it. I think anyone in town would agree with me. You're giving reasons why you fell in love, but that's not the same as admitting you are in love."

"I am not in love!" The crushing feeling in his chest intensified until he wondered how he continued to breathe. Maybe he was having a heart attack. Maybe the situation had pushed him over the edge.

Ethan shook his head. "Answer this question. What would you do if someone tried to harm Amy?"

"That's a stupid question and you know it. I'd fight anyone who tried to hurt her in any way."

"So you care about her?"

"Of course I care about her. Hell, I care about you, although at the moment I can't understand why."

Ethan dismissed his sarcasm with a wave of his hand. "You said you desire, respect, trust and admire her. How many other people do you feel that way about?"

"Well, no one at the moment."

"Face it, Gray. You haven't felt that way about anyone else since I've known you."

"Okay, so she is special. I never denied that."

"She's a special woman who you would do anything to protect, whom you admire, desire, trust, and respect. Face it, man—you are in love."

"You're turning my words against me!"

"No, I'm trying to make you see the light. Love isn't some idealistic aura that spreads around you like magic. It's an everyday thing, a feeling you get when she walks into the room. It's the need you have to be with her, even when you have something else that needs to be done. It's that urge you have to bond with her like no other person, to share private moments and public joys, and yes, even to create a new life that will be the best of you both."

Ethan walked to the door. "Don't tell me you're not in love with Amy. I don't believe you, and for the sake of your happiness, I hope to God she doesn't believe you either."

Gray slumped into a chair by the window, all the fight gone out of him. Ethan couldn't be right...could he?

Chapter Sixteen

She'd been a fool. Ten times a fool. She'd been so certain that a simple pretend dating situation would be harmless. Then she'd convinced herself that she could make love with Gray without being in love with him. Then she'd thought about losing him, only to realize she was in love with him. And after she told him that she wanted all or nothing, he'd been so appalled that he'd shut her out of his life.

You're asking too much, he'd said. No, she wasn't. If she'd never told him how she'd felt, she would be living a lie. Granted, she'd still be by his side, but she would have given herself an ulcer from the tension of holding back her feelings. She couldn't live like that; she deserved more than half a life with the man she loved.

But dammit, who'd decided being right would hurt so much?

Her father stuck his head in her office. ''I'm goin' to the café for lunch. Would you like to come along?''

And endure the pitiful looks of everyone who'd discovered she and Gray were no longer engaged?

"No, thanks Daddy. I'm going to walk over to the house and fix myself a sandwich or something." And try not to think about what a fool I've been.

"Joyce would be mighty glad to see you."

Amy forced herself to smile. "When are you going to make an honest woman out of her?"

Her father jerked upright and he practically sputtered. Twin spots of color spread from his cheeks to his forehead. "We've only been out on a few dates. It's a little early to be hearin' church bells."

His obvious surprise and bluster were a balm to her spirits. She smiled, deciding to push him a little harder. At least one Wheatley should have a successful love life. "Well, neither one of you are getting any younger. I'd get down to business if I were you."

Her father set his lips in a thin line Amy recognized as bullheadedness. He pulled her door closed before limping ever so slightly to lunch.

As soon as he left, she slumped in her chair. She didn't want to see any patients today, much less face friends and family. As a medical doctor, she understood the signs of depression, but this felt more like plain old heartache. The kind of ailment she'd read about in books but never experienced before.

The sound of the front door opening and closing drifted into her consciousness, followed by some conversation she couldn't make out. A walk-in, perhaps, or her father saying goodbye as he left for lunch. She dabbed at her eyes. In either case, she'd better pull herself together. The rest of the day wasn't going to get any easier.

"No, you can't barge in and see her." Amy heard

Gladys' strident voice through the closed door. "Not after you broke her heart."

Broke her heart? She stood on shaky legs and approached the door to her office, pressing her ear to the small crack between the wood and the facing.

"I don't know what's goin' on," she heard her father say, "but I'm pretty sure it's your fault."

Oh, no. They could only be talking to one person. The one person she couldn't see. Not yet. Not until she pulled herself together and could look at him without crying over everything she'd ever wanted, but they never had.

She hadn't even gathered the nerve to return his ring herself.

"I need to talk to her. I tried calling, but that battle-ax of a nurse won't put me through." She imagined Gray addressing her father while pointing to Gladys. He didn't sound like himself at all. The voice she heard through the door was demanding, almost frantic.

He'd tried to call? When? This morning, perhaps. She'd heard the phone ring, but hadn't paid any attention. All her thoughts had been directed inward, exploring her own grief.

"I'm going into that office one way or another," Gray said forcefully.

Amy imagined her father, a fit but older man, standing beside Gladys, who could be a bit intimidating. They might be determined, but they were no match for someone of Gray's age, size and strength. Her hand rested on the knob, torn between wanting to protect her father or her heart.

"Why put her through any more grief?" her father

asked. ''She told me it was through and I'm takin' her at her word.''

''Because she thinks I don't love her!''

''Well, do you?'' her father boldly asked.

''Yes! Yes, I love her.'' A pause punctuated his announcement, then he said louder, ''Amy, do you hear me? I love you.''

Her hand trembled when she opened the door. Standing not six feet away was Gray, flushed and disheveled, his usually neat hair furrowed by fingers of frustration. His leather jacket hung open, revealing a plaid flannel shirt half tucked into jeans. His silvery eyes, normally so calm and cool, were nearly molten with emotion.

''Gray,'' she whispered. ''Are you sure?''

''Yes.'' His gaze devoured her. ''Amy…yes.''

Tears pooled in her eyes until the scene before her wavered and blurred. She opened her arms, and then Gray was there, holding her so tight she thought they might fuse into one.

He leaned back enough to look into her eyes, then lowered his head and kissed her. Hard and sweet and demanding, the kiss was everything she'd wanted. Commitment, love, trust and a promise of the future. She slanted her head and kissed him back, telling him everything without saying a word.

Gradually, she heard a sniffle, then a gentle cough. Breaking apart, she looked around Gray's shoulder at her father and Gladys. ''If it's okay with you, I think I will take my lunch break now,'' she said.

''Fine,'' he father said. ''I didn't need to go to the café anyway. You take all the time you want.''

"I'll reschedule anything you need," Gladys said, her voice vibrating with what Amy hoped was joy.

"Good," Gray said, "because we have some talking to do and I'm not very good before an audience."

"Since when," Amy asked. "You seemed to do pretty well when you proposed in the restaurant in Wimberley."

"This time it's for real...and forever."

Her arms held him tight as tears escaped her eyes and ran down her cheeks, wetting his soft flannel shirt. He didn't seem to mind. He stroked her hair and held her in return.

Moments passed. The tears stopped, and in their place, an impatience to hear and touch and experience all that Gray wanted to share.

"Let's go next door to my house."

"I have a better idea. Let's go to mine."

Amy nodded. She turned to her father and Gladys. "Can you handle my patients?"

"For this? Of course we can. Now get on out of here before the two of you embarrass a couple of senior citizens."

Gladys swatted her father on his arm. "Speak for yourself, you old coot."

Amy and Gray both laughed as they headed outside. A gleaming silver luxury sports-utility vehicle was parked in front of the clinic.

"The dealer delivered it this morning," he explained as he opened her door. "I wanted something a little bigger, a little more of a family vehicle."

"A family?"

"Yeah," he said, a very uncharacteristic grin on

his face. "I think that would be nice, whenever you're ready."

Instead of heading toward his house, they set out north. "Where are we going?"

"Back to where this started," he said, his hands firm on the wheel. "I want to be alone with you at the cabin. Can you wait that long?"

Amy nodded, but she wasn't sure she could be patient. The drive seemed to take forever. Much of the landscape was unfamiliar because when they'd driven to the cabin from Austin she'd been asleep, and the darkness had obscured any landmarks. Now, in the bright winter sun, the lake gleamed a brilliant blue.

Gray pulled the SUV to a stop in front of the cabin, but Amy didn't wait for him to come around to her side. She jumped down and met him in front. With a smile, he took her hand. "I would carry you across the threshold, but my doctor would probably tell me that's bad for my knee."

"Save it for the honeymoon," she said, then stopped. "That is, I assume..."

Gray laughed, the joyous sound seeming to reverberate across the low hills surrounding the lake. "Let me do this one my way, okay? No pressure from friends and neighbors, no family expectations, no other reason than the right one."

"And that is?"

"Inside," he said, a gleam in his eyes she understood.

He unlocked the door, then kissed her as they crossed the threshold. When she opened her eyes, they were standing in the living room of the modest, cozy cabin where Gray had fixed breakfast for her months before.

He tugged her over to the couch, which was an overstuffed piece covered in a colorful red-and-brown woven throw. Sinking down together, he kissed her again, his hands framing her face. When he pulled back, he smiled. ''You are so beautiful.''

''Even a bit tearstained and blotchy?''

''Even then. I assume I'm the cause of the tears, right?''

''There were tears of sorrow, then tears of joy. Both for you.''

''Then I'm sorry and I'm glad,'' he said, pushing her hair back from her cheek. ''I'm sorry I didn't realize the truth until sometime in the wee hours of the morning. I'm glad you were willing to listen, that you hadn't given up on me.''

''I don't think I could ever give up on you, Gray. I love you.''

He looked deep into her eyes, his expression so intense she breath seemed frozen in her lungs. ''I love you too, with all my heart.''

''Oh, Gray,'' she whispered, reaching for him, holding him tight once more as though she were afraid he might vanish. He wouldn't, she knew. Gray was steady and purposeful and he never made commitments lightly. If he said he loved her, she believed him one hundred percent.

''I want us to get married, just like we'd planned, with our family and friends looking on. I want to have a family with you and watch our children grow up in this small town we both love. I want to grow old with you, and love you until I draw my last breath.''

''What made you change your mind?'' She had to know, to understand how this man of deep convictions had reversed his thinking so quickly.

''Ethan came to see me. It seems your father recruited him to speak to me, since we're friends. He basically called me a damned fool because I didn't recognize what was right before me all along. I loved you, but I was afraid to put a name to it. I was afraid that if I said the word, I was condemning myself to suffer again. I had to let go of the past, of the problems of my first marriage and the bad examples I'd witnessed in my childhood to see the truth.''

''And what is the truth?''

''That you and I have many things in common, but we're two separate people. That we draw strength from each other, yet provide support when we need it. That together we are much better than either of us would be apart.''

''And love?''

''I don't know how to define it as eloquently as Ethan did when he made me face my past, but now I recognize love for what it is. The feeling I get when I think of you, look at you. The contentment our relationship brings, the joy you give to me every day. I could live without it, but I'd never be happy.''

He framed her face again and looked deep into her soul. ''And I want to be happy with you, and make you happy, for all our days. Will you marry me, Dr. Amy Wheatley, in sickness and in health, 'til death us do part?''

"Yes," she whispered, emotion clogging her voice, stinging her eyes. "A thousand times yes."

He slipped the emerald-cut diamond back on her finger. "This time, it's forever."

THE WEDDING TOOK PLACE on a cloudless day in June, just as Amy had planned, with nearly a hundred of their friends, family and neighbors looking on. Gray stood at the gazebo where the ceremony would occur and looked out over the crowd. His mother and stepfather had dressed as though they were attending a more formal indoor wedding. They must be uncomfortable in the lingering heat of the day, but did their best to appear unfazed by ninety-degree temperatures and persistent, buzzing insects.

His father and his new wife—Gray refused to think of the thirty-something former actress/model as his stepmother—sat one row back, looking considerably more comfortable. His dad wore a pale linen unstructured suit and his wife wore a very short, very sleeveless sheath with high, strappy gold sandals that had gotten stuck in the turf on several occasions. Her high-pitched giggles had caused a few heads to turn in the conservative community of Ranger Springs.

Friends from Dallas, Austin and Gray's new hometown filled out several rows of folding chairs, along with some business associates. A very pregnant Robin sat on the end of a row so she could dash to the ladies' room as needed. A common occurrence, Ethan had explained with a grin. His beloved aunt, who now lived in Houston, sat beside Robin to keep her company...just in case the baby decided to make an early entrance.

And on the other side, Ambrose Wheatley's new bride, Joyce, sat next to her husband's chair, where he would sit after walking his daughter down the aisle. Ambrose and Joyce had surprised everyone by eloping to Las Vegas one day in early May. They didn't want to interfere with Amy's wedding, they'd explained, and besides, they weren't getting any younger. They seemed to get a "big kick" out of the Elvis impersonator conducting their ceremony on the Strip. Amy couldn't be happier for them.

Thelma sat next to Joyce and Gina Summers. She'd better watch out, or the merry matchmakers would be fixing her up next. Encouraged by their success, they wouldn't be happy until all the single people in town had found their perfect mates.

The organ music continued to play. Gray shifted as a bead of sweat rolled down his back, well hidden by the gray tuxedo he wore. Wasn't it time for the ceremony to begin? He was all packed and ready to start the honeymoon—a two-week cruise with a private balcony and a king-size bed. He'd taken a big step and groomed his management team to take over for him. There wasn't anything they couldn't handle—with just a few phone calls from him occasionally to make sure his "baby" was running smoothly.

"Do you remember what you said last year?" Ethan asked.

"About what?"

"When I was standing here waiting for Robin to walk down the aisle?"

"Not really," Gray said. It was the truth; he couldn't recall the exact words.

"If I remember correctly, I predicted you'd be

standing up here one day, and you said something about 'when pigs fly.' Well, I'm waiting for the flying pigs."

Gray shrugged. "So I was wrong." He'd have to remember to find a souvenir with a flying pig to bring back to his friend.

"I'm glad you can admit it. Now, if everyone knew you'd actually made a mistake, you wouldn't have such as reputation as being perfect."

"I never claimed to be perfect." In fact, he and Amy had talked about his tendency to show a "perfect" facade to the world. With her help he'd come to understand how his childhood had made him into the man he was today. For the first time in his life, he felt free to show Amy the real Grayson Phillips, without fear she'd think less of him if he weren't everyone's ideal friend, son, business associate and now husband.

"No? Then what was all that 'best blind date' stuff I used to hear about?"

"All in my past," Gray said, his attention tuned to the front of Bretford House, where Amy would make her march down the aisle. "The only dates I'll be going on in the future are with my wife."

"Good attitude," Ethan advised as the wedding march began.

Amy walked down the pale lavender carpet, a vision in white lace and seed pearls. The simple lines of her gown were complemented by a full veil that fluttered in the light breeze. Even this far away, he could see her blue eyes glistening with tears. When she walked closer, he smelled her soft perfume. When she stood before him, he took her hands.

"Hello, Dr. Amy Jo Wheatley. I'm going to be your date for this evening...and for the rest of our lives."

HARLEQUIN WALK DOWN THE AISLE TO MAUI CONTEST 1197
OFFICIAL RULES
NO PURCHASE NECESSARY TO ENTER

1. To enter, follow directions published in the offer to which you are responding. Contest begins April 2, 2001, and ends on October 1, 2001. Method of entry may vary. Mailed entries must be postmarked by October 1, 2001, and received by October 8, 2001.
2. Contest entry may be, at times, presented via the Internet, but will be restricted solely to residents of certain georgraphic areas that are disclosed on the Web site. To enter via the Internet, if permissible, access the Harlequin Web site (www.eHarlequin.com) and follow the directions displayed online. Online entries must be received by 11:59 p.m. E.S.T. on October 1, 2001.

   In lieu of submitting an entry online, enter by mail by hand-printing (or typing) on an 8½" x 11" plain piece of paper, your name, address (including zip code), Contest number/name and in 250 words or fewer, why winning a Harlequin wedding dress would make your wedding day special. Mail via first-class mail to: Harlequin Walk Down the Aisle Contest 1197, (in the U.S.) P.O. Box 9076, 3010 Walden Avenue, Buffalo, NY 14269-9076, (in Canada) P.O. Box 637, Fort Erie, Ontario L2A 5X3, Canada.

   Limit one entry per person, household address and e-mail address. Online and/or mailed entries received from persons residing in geographic areas in which Internet entry is not permissible will be disqualified.
3. Contests will be judged by a panel of members of the Harlequin editorial, marketing and public relations staff based on the following criteria:
   - Originality and Creativity—50%
   - Emotionally Compelling—25%
   - Sincerity—25%

   In the event of a tie, duplicate prizes will be awarded. Decisions of the judges are final.
4. All entries become the property of Torstar Corp. and will not be returned. No responsibility is assumed for lost, late, illegible, incomplete, inaccurate, nondelivered or misdirected mail or misdirected e-mail, for technical, hardware or software failures of any kind, lost or unavailable network connections, or failed, incomplete, garbled or delayed computer transmission or any human error which may occur in the receipt or processing of the entries in this Contest.
5. Contest open only to residents of the U.S. (except Puerto Rico) and Canada, who are 18 years of age or older, and is void wherever prohibited by law; all applicable laws and regulations apply. Any litigation within the Provice of Quebec respecting the conduct or organization of a publicity contest may be submitted to the Régie des alcools, des courses et des jeux for a ruling. Any litigation respecting the awarding of a prize may be submitted to the Régie des alcools, des courses et des jeux only for the purpose of helping the parties reach a settlement. Employees and immediate family members of Torstar Corp. and D. L. Blair, Inc., their affiliates, subsidiaries and all other agencies, entities and persons connected with the use, marketing or conduct of this Contest are not eligible to enter. Taxes on prizes are the sole responsibility of winners. Acceptance of any prize offered constitutes permission to use winner's name, photograph or other likeness for the purposes of advertising, trade and promotion on behalf of Torstar Corp., its affiliates and subsidiaries without further compensation to the winner, unless prohibited by law.
6. Winners will be determined no later than November 15, 2001, and will be notified by mail. Winners will be required to sign and return an Affidavit of Eligibility form within 15 days after winner notification. Noncompliance within that time period may result in disqualification and an alternative winner may be selected. Winners of trip must execute a Release of Liability prior to ticketing and must possess required travel documents (e.g. passport, photo ID) where applicable. Trip must be completed by November 2002. No substitution of prize permitted by winner. Torstar Corp. and D. L. Blair, Inc., their parents, affiliates, and subsidiaries are not responsible for errors in printing or electronic presentation of Contest, entries and/or game pieces. In the event of printing or other errors which may result in unintended prize values or duplication of prizes, all affected game pieces or entries shall be null and void. If for any reason the Internet portion of the Contest is not capable of running as planned, including infection by computer virus, bugs, tampering, unauthorized intervention, fraud, technical failures, or any other causes beyond the control of Torstar Corp. which corrupt or affect the administration, secrecy, fairness, integrity or proper conduct of the Contest, Torstar Corp. reserves the right, at its sole discretion, to disqualify any individual who tampers with the entry process and to cancel, terminate, modify or suspend the Contest or the Internet portion thereof. In the event of a dispute regarding an online entry, the entry will be deemed submitted by the authorized holder of the e-mail account submitted at the time of entry. Authorized account holder is defined as the natural person who is assigned to an e-mail address by an Internet access provider, online service provider or other organization that is responsible for arranging e-mail address for the domain associated with the submitted e-mail address. **Purchase or acceptance of a product offer does not improve your chances of winning.**
7. Prizes: (1) Grand Prize—A Harlequin wedding dress (approximate retail value: $3,500) and a 5-night/6-day honeymoon trip to Maui, HI, including round-trip air transportation provided by Maui Visitors Bureau from Los Angeles International Airport (winner is responsible for transportation to and from Los Angeles International Airport) and a Harlequin Romance Package, including hotel accomodations (double occupancy) at the Hyatt Regency Maui Resort and Spa, dinner for (2) two at Swan Court, a sunset sail on Kiele V and a spa treatment for the winner (approximate retail value: $4,000); (5) Five runner-up prizes of a $1000 gift certificate to selected retail outlets to be determined by Sponsor (retail value $1000 ea.). Prizes consist of only those items listed as part of the prize. Limit one prize per person. All prizes are valued in U.S. currency.
8. For a list of winners (available after December 17, 2001) send a self-addressed, stamped envelope to: Harlequin Walk Down the Aisle Contest 1197 Winners, P.O. Box 4200 Blair, NE 68009-4200 or you may access the www.eHarlequin.com Web site through January 15, 2002.

Contest sponsored by Torstar Corp., P.O. Box 9042, Buffalo, NY 14269-9042, U.S.A.

PHWDACONT2